THE GOBLIN KING

ALAYA JOHNSON

ILLUSTRATED BY MEG GANDY

GRAPHIC UNIVERSE ™ · MINNEAPOLIS · NEW YORK

Story by Alaya Johnson

Pencils and inks by Meg Gandy

Coloring by Hi-Fi Design

Lettering by Marshall Dillon

Copyright © 2009 by Lerner Publishing Group, Inc.

Graphic Universe™ is a trademark and Twisted Journeys® is a registered trademark
of Lerner Publishing Group, Inc.

Graphic Universe
A division of Lerner Publishing Group, Inc.
241 First Avenue North
Minneapolis, MN 55401 U.S.A.

Website address: www.lernerbooks.com

Library of Congress Cataloging-in-Publication Data

Johnson, Alaya Dawn, 1982–
    The Goblin King / by Alaya Johnson ; illustrated by Meg Gandy.
        p.   cm. — (Twisted journeys)
    Summary: Throughout this graphic novel about a student taken into fairyland
while on a trip to Scotland's Orkney Islands, the reader makes choices to determine
the outcome of the fairies' battle with the Goblin King, as well as the hero's fate.
    ISBN: 978–0–8225–9253–2 (lib. bdg. : alk. paper)
    1. Graphic novels. [1. Graphic novels. 2. Fairies—Fiction. 3. Goblins—Fiction.
4. Imaginary creatures—Fiction. 5. Animals, Mythical—Fiction. 6. Plot-your-own
stories. 7. Orkney (Scotland)—Fiction. 8. Scotland—Fiction.] I. Gandy, Meg, ill.
II. Title.
PZ7.7.J64Gob 2009
[Fic]—dc22   2007049001

Manufactured in the United States of America
1 2 3 4 5 6 – DP – 14 13 12 11 10 09

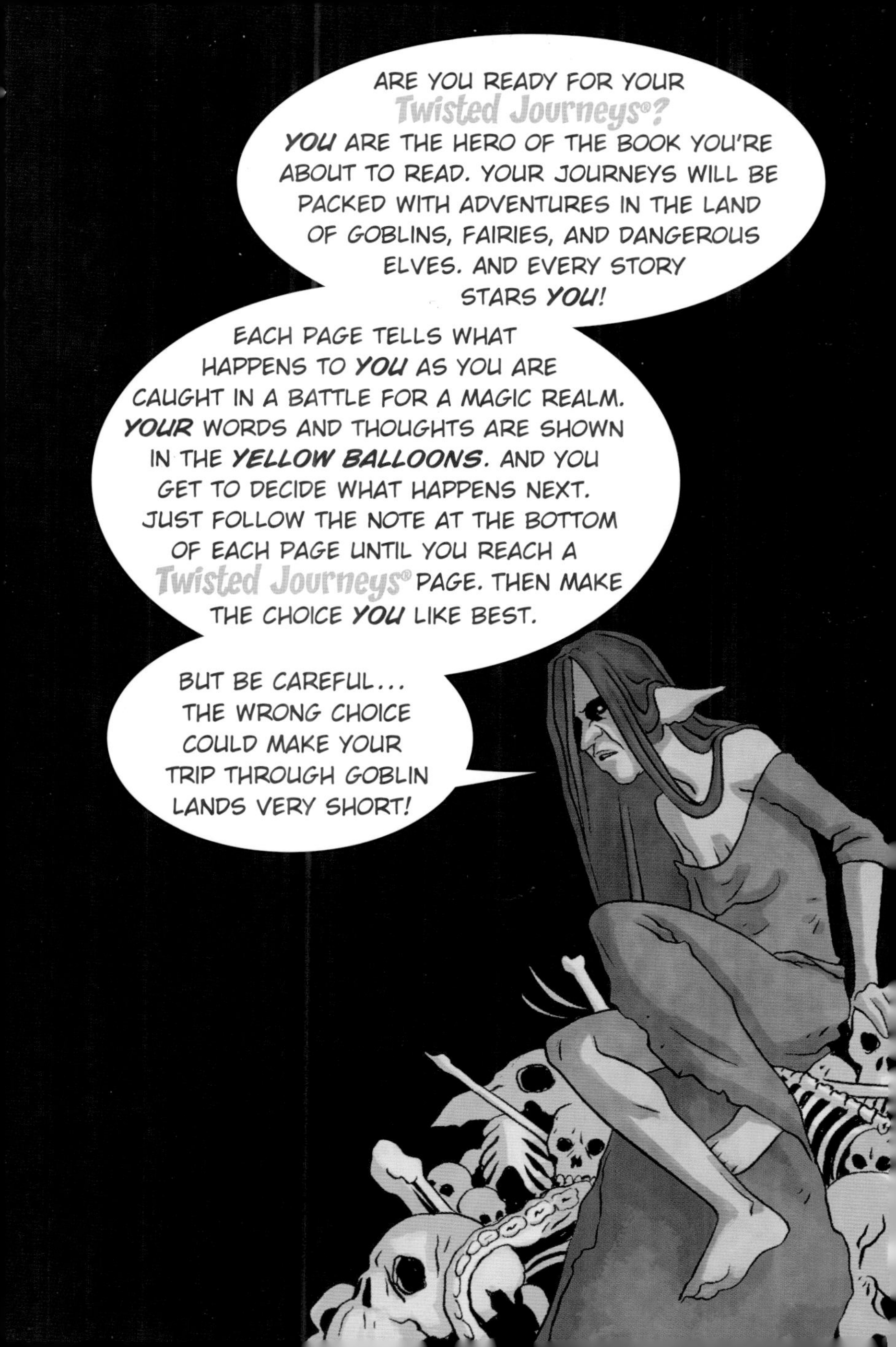
ARE YOU READY FOR YOUR Twisted Journeys®? YOU ARE THE HERO OF THE BOOK YOU'RE ABOUT TO READ. YOUR JOURNEYS WILL BE PACKED WITH ADVENTURES IN THE LAND OF GOBLINS, FAIRIES, AND DANGEROUS ELVES. AND EVERY STORY STARS YOU!
EACH PAGE TELLS WHAT HAPPENS TO YOU AS YOU ARE CAUGHT IN A BATTLE FOR A MAGIC REALM. YOUR WORDS AND THOUGHTS ARE SHOWN IN THE YELLOW BALLOONS. AND YOU GET TO DECIDE WHAT HAPPENS NEXT. JUST FOLLOW THE NOTE AT THE BOTTOM OF EACH PAGE UNTIL YOU REACH A Twisted Journeys® PAGE. THEN MAKE THE CHOICE YOU LIKE BEST.
BUT BE CAREFUL... THE WRONG CHOICE COULD MAKE YOUR TRIP THROUGH GOBLIN LANDS VERY SHORT!

You can't believe it—you and ten other students have won a trip to Scotland! You've always wanted to go, and now you're on a ferry to the island of Rousay in Orkney.

The sea is gentle. In the distance, you see sleek brown animals jumping in the waves. You lean over the railing of the ferryboat and point. "What are those?" you ask.

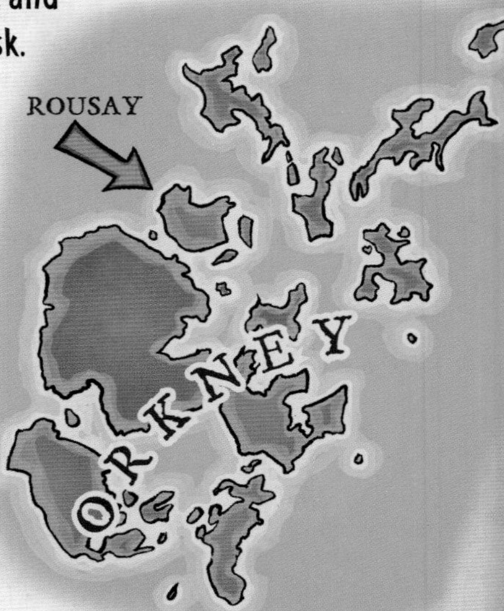
ROUSAY
ORKNEY

Ms. Fraser, your group leader, smiles behind her thick glasses. "Och, those are seals," she says in her strong Scottish accent. "Some folk around here would say they're selkies."

"What's a selkie?" asks one of the other students.

"Why, they're one of the fair folk," she says. "Scotland has all sorts."

"Fair folk?" you ask. "You mean fairies?"

Ms. Fraser nods. "And you had best be careful around them. You wouldn't want to get stolen by a hobgoblin or invited to a fairy feast, now would you? You might never leave!"

GO ON TO THE NEXT PAGE.

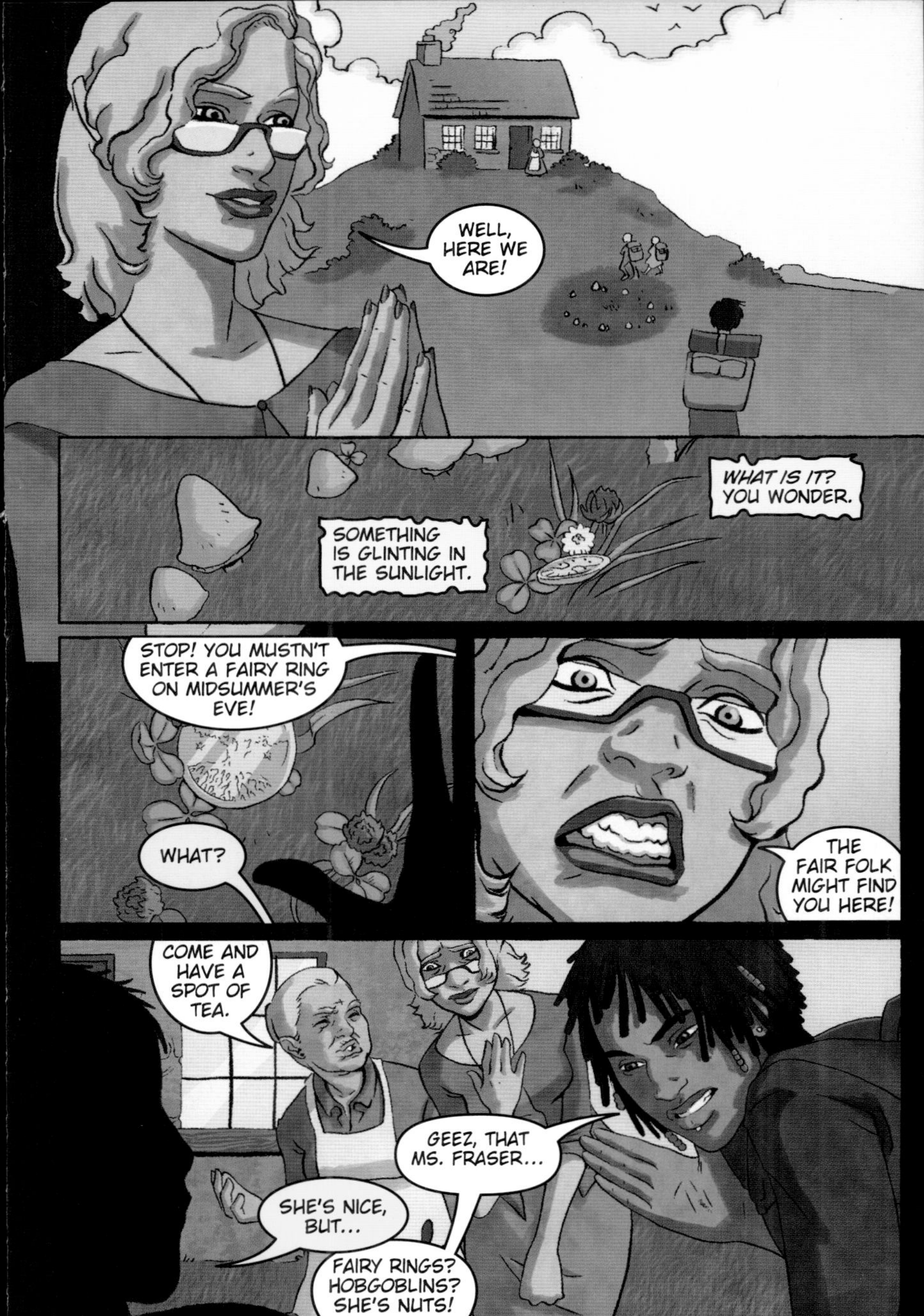
WELL, HERE WE ARE!
SOMETHING IS GLINTING IN THE SUNLIGHT.
WHAT IS IT? YOU WONDER.
STOP! YOU MUSTN'T ENTER A FAIRY RING ON MIDSUMMER'S EVE!
WHAT?
THE FAIR FOLK MIGHT FIND YOU HERE!
COME AND HAVE A SPOT OF TEA.
GEEZ, THAT MS. FRASER...
SHE'S NICE, BUT...
FAIRY RINGS? HOBGOBLINS? SHE'S NUTS!

GO ON TO THE NEXT PAGE.

Okay, so maybe Ms. Fraser *is* a bit . . . odd. But could those old legends really be true after all? *Should* you have left that strange silver coin in the fairy ring?

Soon enough, night falls, and you and the other students go to your rooms to sleep. Outside your window, the ocean waves crash against the rocks with a noise as loud as thunder. You try to sleep, but it's hard. The wind is howling. The more you listen, the more it sounds as though someone is speaking.

"Come to us," you hear.

You put the pillow over your head. But the voice won't leave you alone.

"We know you're there," it says. "Come outside."

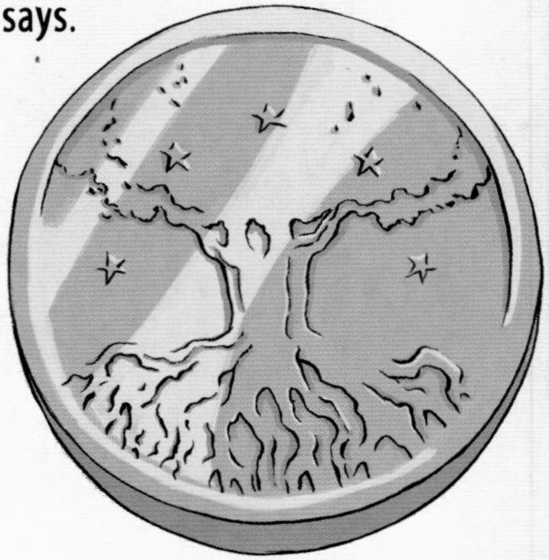

The wind can't speak. You know that. But just in case, you walk to the window.

You gasp. A fairy is floating in the middle of the mushroom circle.

Maybe you shouldn't have taken that coin.

GO ON TO THE NEXT PAGE.

Crazy Ms. Fraser was right—the legends are true!
You feel a little excited, but scared too.
Fairies can be dangerous.

WILL YOU...

. . . wake up Ms. Fraser?
She ought to know what to do.
TURN TO PAGE 41.

. . . go outside and see what the fairy wants?
TURN TO PAGE 48.

"Puck."

Queen Titania claps her hands. "Poor Puck, the babe has won!"

"Not yet," Puck says. "To lead an army, one must be able to ask as well as answer."

"What a sore loser," you mutter.

"Who said that?" Puck demands. He turns around and starts to sprint in your direction. You cover your head, but just before it seems he will knock you and the nearest fairies to the floor, he floats up high above.

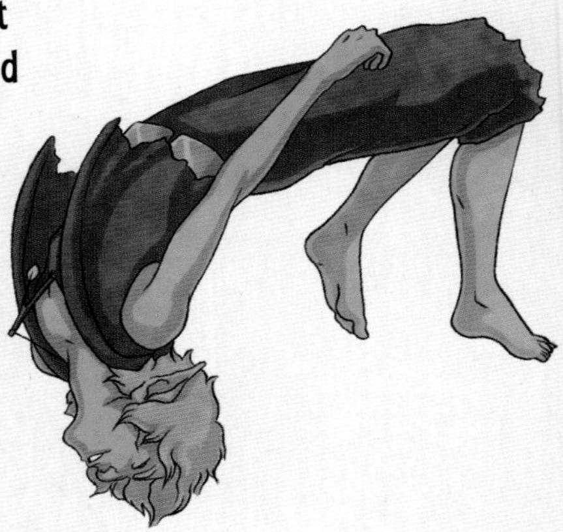

"How many babes can do this?" he shouts. "Who do you think should lead our army?"

Most of the fairies cheer him, but Titania looks annoyed.

"Puck, come down at once. Fine, let the child ask you a question. But if you get it wrong, let no one say I was not fair."

Puck floats back down to the ground like a giant feather. "My pleasure," he says. He turns to you. "Well, then? What can you ask that I don't know?"

GO ON TO THE NEXT PAGE.

You just need a good riddle, right?
Or maybe something simple would work better.

WILL YOU...

. . . ask him what your name is?
TURN TO PAGE 86.

. . . ask a riddle?
TURN TO PAGE 59.

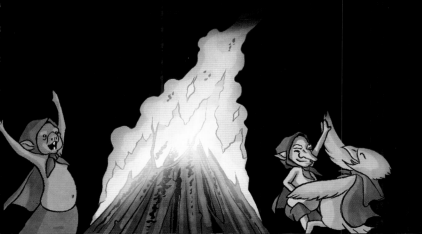

"I'll join your army," you say. "But I'm just a frog. Won't you change me back first?"

"I welcome any creature into my army," says Robin. "Even frogs."

"Why are you fighting the fairies, anyway?" you ask.

The king sits on his trash heap. "Why? Because the fairies have no care for any other creatures but themselves. They think of us as their servants and slaves. They look down on us because we live in the houses of humans. I used to serve King Oberon and Queen Titania. We're fighting this battle to prove we're their equals!"

The goblins around you let out a roar.

"And we'll defeat that traitor, Puck!" says a nearby goblin.

The king jumps up. "Puck will learn how strong we are!"

"Who is Puck?" you ask the goblin.

"A servant of the fairy queen. He betrayed our king and turned him into a changeling baby."

"It's time!" yells the king. "Tonight, we win!"

GO ON TO THE NEXT PAGE.

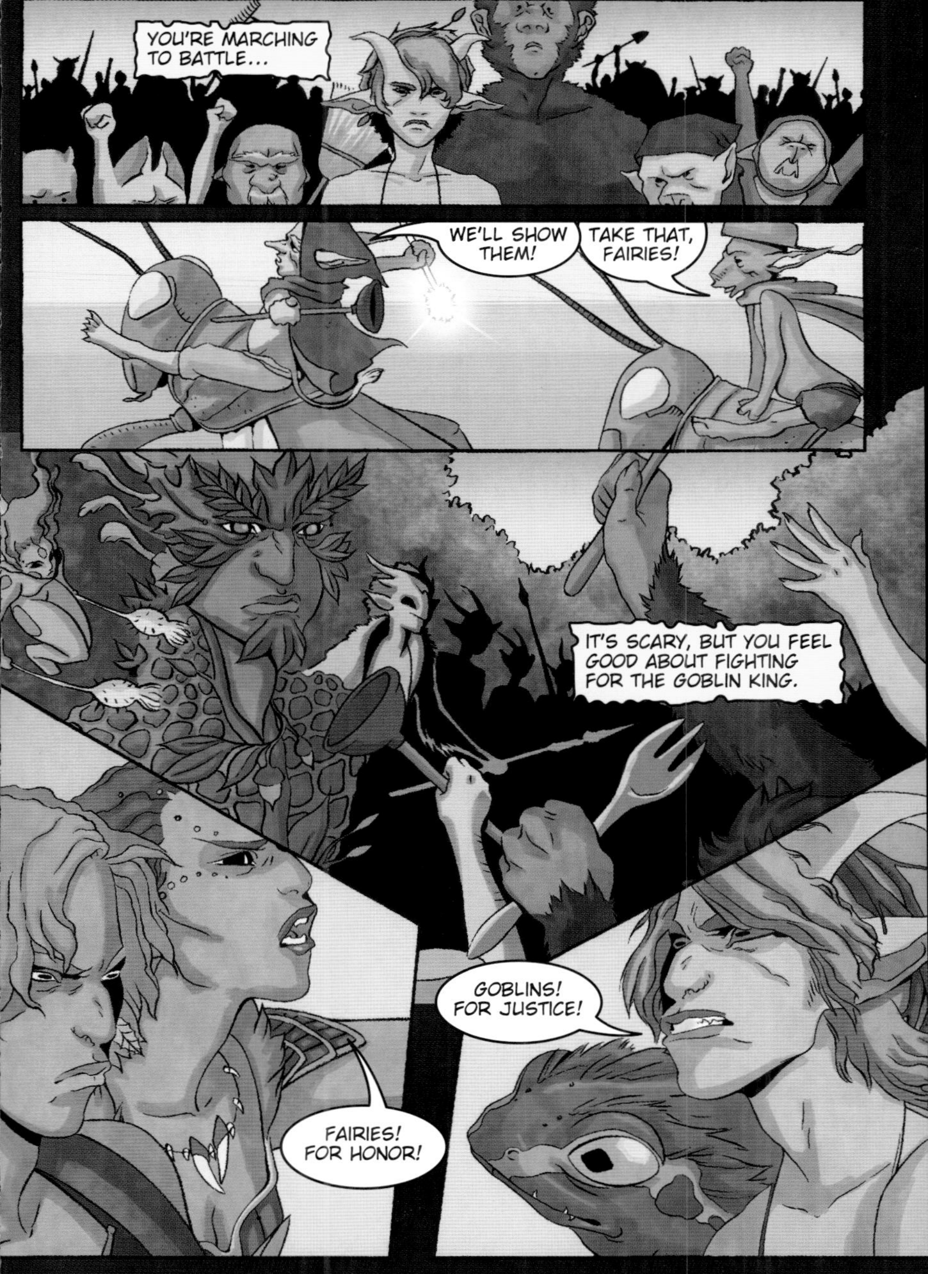
YOU'RE MARCHING TO BATTLE...
WE'LL SHOW THEM!
TAKE THAT, FAIRIES!
IT'S SCARY, BUT YOU FEEL GOOD ABOUT FIGHTING FOR THE GOBLIN KING.
GOBLINS! FOR JUSTICE!
FAIRIES! FOR HONOR!

GO ON TO THE NEXT PAGE.

All around you, the goblin army rushes forward. You race to keep up with Robin Goodfellow. Since your frog body can't hold a weapon, you figure that you're probably the safest with him. Screams and gurgles and shouts surround you. You try not to look, but it's hard to avoid seeing the horribly wounded.

"Puck!" yells Robin Goodfellow above the noise.

As if by magic, a short elf that you recognize from the fairy court appears before him. "You wanted me, Robin?" says Puck.

"Shall we settle this?" the Goblin King says.

"With pleasure," says Puck. With a loud clash of weapons, they begin to fight. You see something familiar in the corner of your eye and turn to look. You can't believe it: someone who looks *exactly* like you is marching in the fairy army.

Puck laughs, and you turn back around. He's holding a branch with vines growing out of it . . . and the vines are strangling Robin Goodfellow!

GO ON TO THE NEXT PAGE.

Should you try to save the Goblin King? That stick Puck is using could be the Ever-Blooming Branch that you refused to get for Titania. Or maybe you should find the fairy who looks like you before it gets away.

WILL YOU...

... try to knock the branch from Puck's hand and save Robin Goodfellow?
TURN TO PAGE 80.

... chase after your mysterious twin?
TURN TO PAGE 55.

... stand back and wait to see how the battle goes?
TURN TO PAGE 43.

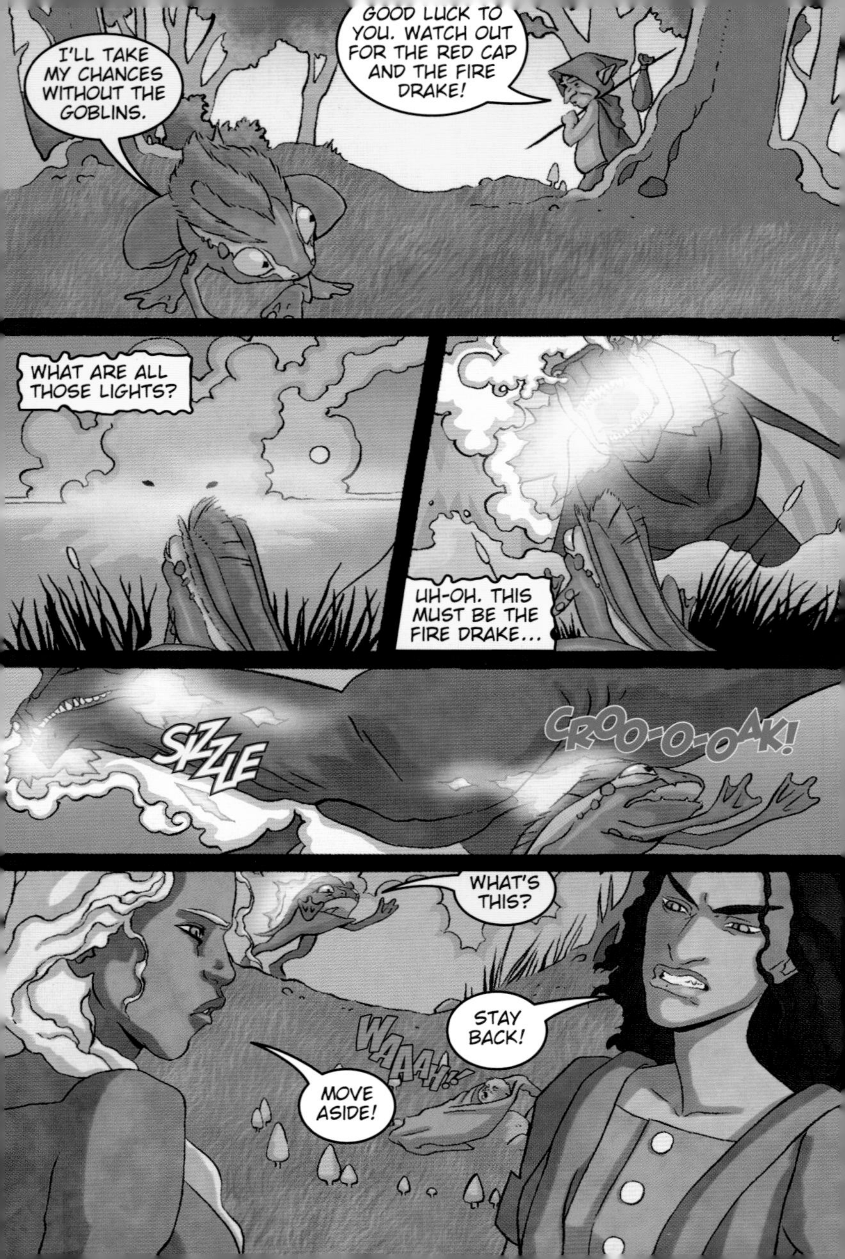
I'LL TAKE MY CHANCES WITHOUT THE GOBLINS.
GOOD LUCK TO YOU. WATCH OUT FOR THE RED CAP AND THE FIRE DRAKE!
WHAT ARE ALL THOSE LIGHTS?
UH-OH. THIS MUST BE THE FIRE DRAKE...
SIZZLE
CROO-O-OAK!
WHAT'S THIS?
STAY BACK!
WAAAH!
MOVE ASIDE!

As soon as you escape the fire drake, you hear a baby crying. What is a human baby doing in Tir na nOg? You hop closer to the sound and see the baby lying on the grass in the center of a fairy ring. Nearby, two beautiful women fight each other with heavy branches. One of the women has hair like pure gold, while the other's hair is black as a crow's feathers. They put down their weapons when you come closer.

"I can't enter the fairy ring," says the golden one. "Will you go in and get the baby for me, traveler?"

"No," says the other, "you must give him to me!"

You consider. "If I help, which of you will turn me back into a human?"

The first one smiles. "I have that power."

The dark-haired one just frowns. "She's a liar. Only I can."

You look back at the baby. Its fate is in your hands now.

GO ON TO THE NEXT PAGE.

These women are mysterious.
Should you give *either* of them the baby?
What if this is just a trap?

WILL YOU...

...get the baby and give it to the
golden-haired lady?
TURN TO PAGE 35.

...get the baby and give it to
the crow-haired lady?
TURN TO PAGE 53.

...get the baby and run
away with it?
TURN TO PAGE 44.

...leave the women and the baby alone?
You can't trust anyone here.
TURN TO PAGE 107.

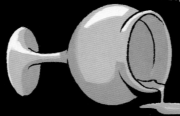

You swim away, wincing as the sea trows howl behind you.

"Cousin will be angry!"

"Come back, come back!"

They try to chase after you, but you swim to the sandy bottom and cover your head with a large clamshell. Once they leave, you drop the shell and look around. Are those buildings you see in the distance? Excited, you start to swim toward them. It takes much too long, since your feet aren't nearly as useful as flippers. You're panting by the time you get close to the huge city made out of coral and sand. Dozens of mermaids swim below you.

"A brownie spoon!" a girl exclaims.

You turn around and see a young mermaid with a purple tail and jewels in her hair.

"I've always wanted one," she says. "You have to give it to me!"

"Sorry," you say. "I can't."

The girl pouts. "Well then. My mummy will just have to punish you."

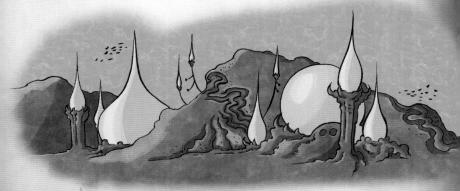

GO ON TO THE NEXT PAGE.

"Your mummy?" you ask.

The girl puts her hands on her hips. "She's the queen."

Uh-oh. Before you can swim away—*fast*—she grabs you by the wrist. She's stronger than she looks. She manages to drag you all the way to a palace made of crystal and coral. An older mermaid with red hair and a coral crown swims from inside it.

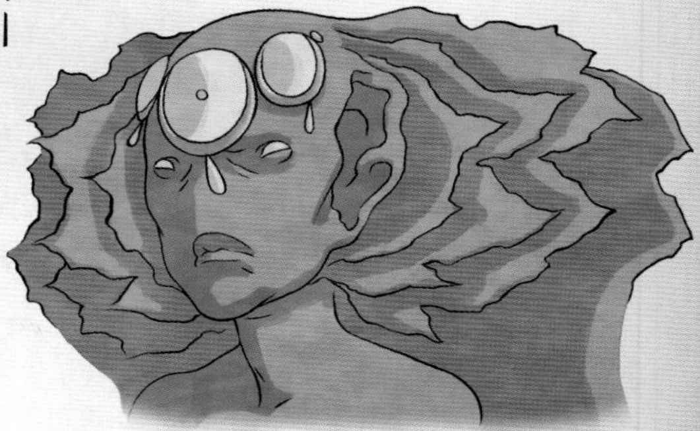

"What's the matter, daughter?"

"This evil human promised me the brownie spoon but won't give it to me!"

The queen frowns. "You shouldn't promise what you won't give, human."

"But . . . but I never promised!" you splutter. "I need this spoon!"

The queen considers. "What is it worth to you?"

Suddenly you get an idea. "The Kelpie kidnapped my teacher. If you can save her, the spoon is yours."

She nods solemnly. "But to have our royal help, you must prove your merit. If you answer this riddle correctly, I will save your teacher."

GO ON TO THE NEXT PAGE.

There's a wee house
And it's full of meat
But neither door nor window
Will let you in to eat.

IS IT...

...an egg?
TURN TO PAGE 72

...a clam?
TURN TO PAGE 101.

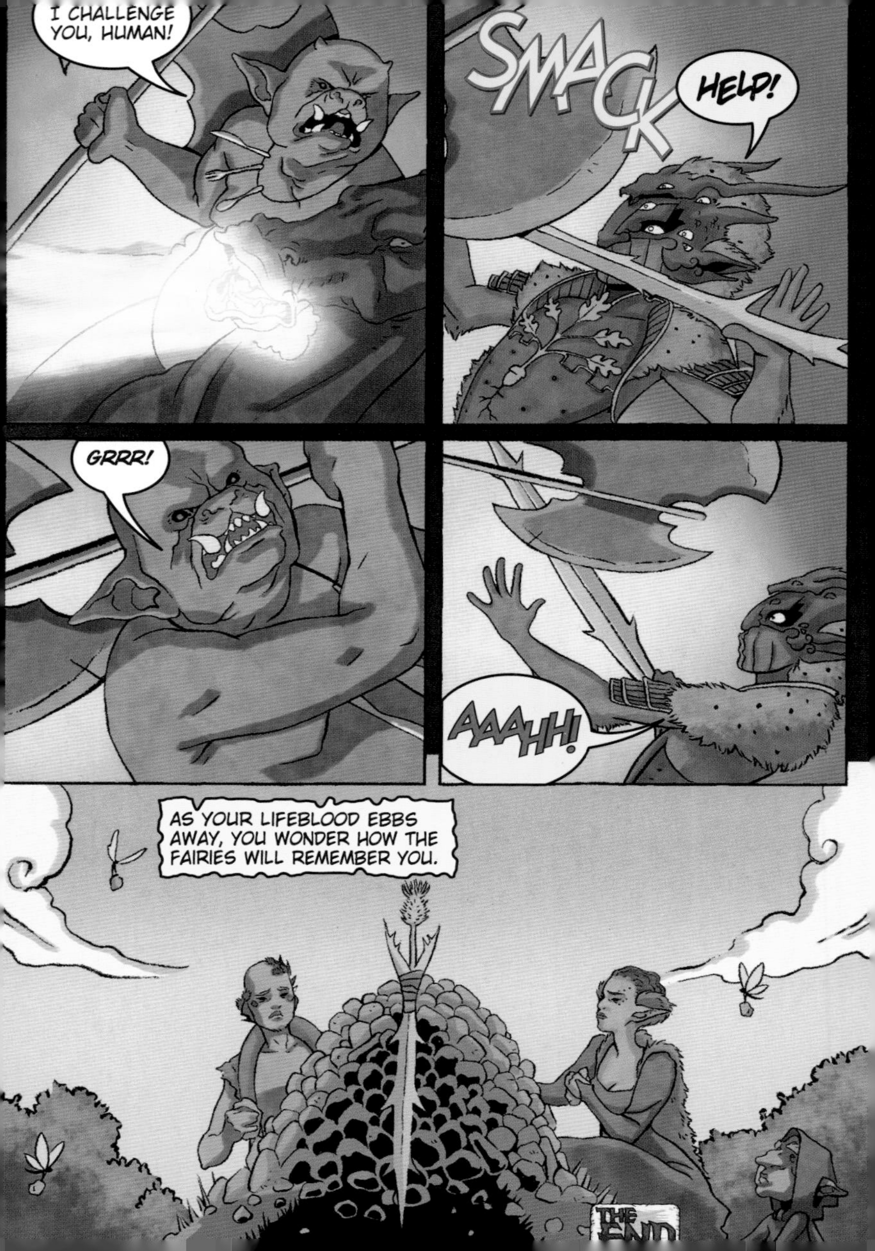
I CHALLENGE YOU, HUMAN!
SMACK
HELP!
GRRR!
AAAHH!
AS YOUR LIFEBLOOD EBBS AWAY, YOU WONDER HOW THE FAIRIES WILL REMEMBER YOU.
THE END

The army of little mushrooms takes you deeper and deeper into the tunnels. Soon you can't tell how long you've been following them underground. Days? Months? Your stomach rumbles. Before you can stop yourself, you grab a few of the little mushrooms and stuff them in your mouth. Yum. You've always liked mushrooms. As soon as you swallow them, you feel your body change from a frog back into a human. How lucky! The mushrooms lead you even deeper into the tunnel maze.

They let you sleep sometimes, but you never see the outside. Eventually, you forget what grass smells like and how the sun felt on your skin. You grow taller. Your hair starts to touch your knees. Your clothes turn to rags. Every time you eat one mushroom, the others multiply to fill its place.

The mushrooms never seem to run out of tunnels to explore, but you never do find the Goblin King.

THE END

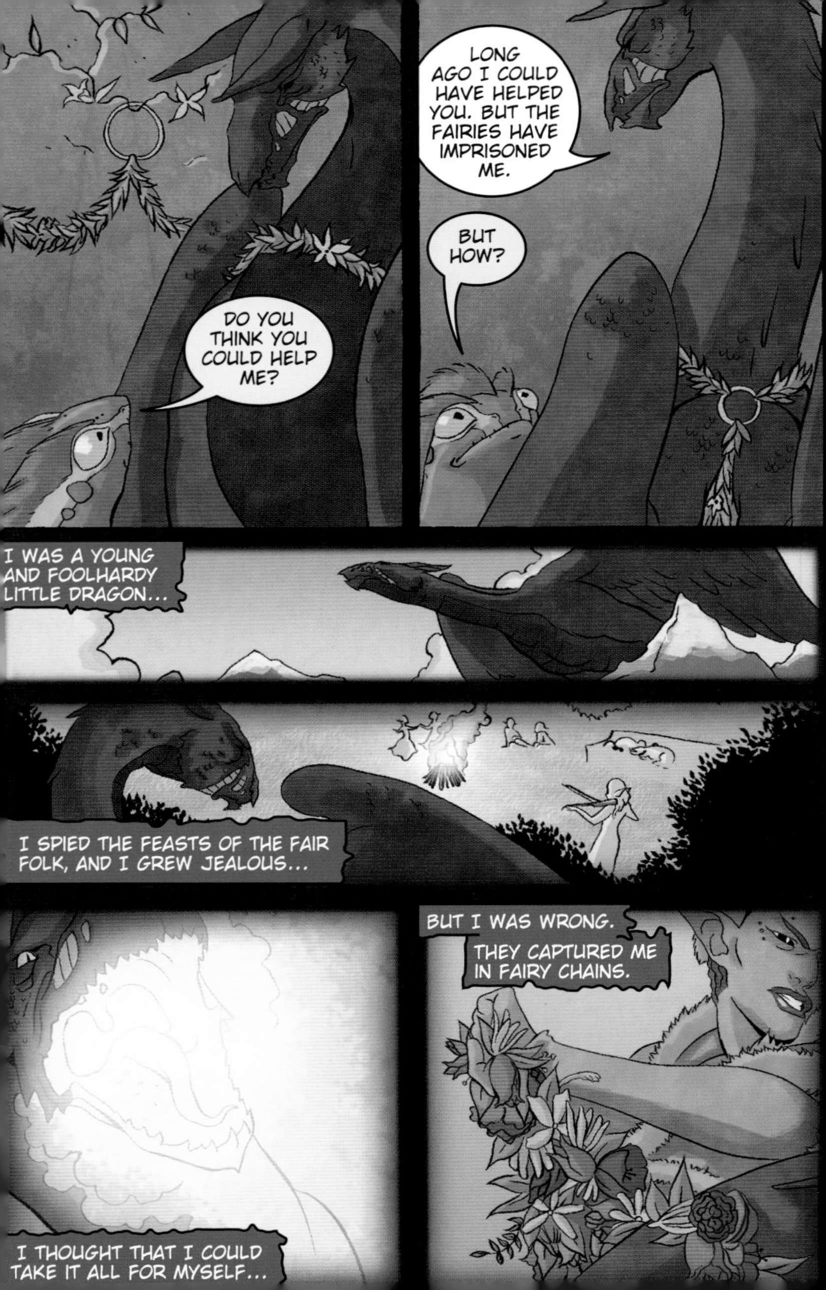
DO YOU THINK YOU COULD HELP ME?
LONG AGO I COULD HAVE HELPED YOU. BUT THE FAIRIES HAVE IMPRISONED ME.
BUT HOW?
I WAS A YOUNG AND FOOLHARDY LITTLE DRAGON...
I SPIED THE FEASTS OF THE FAIR FOLK, AND I GREW JEALOUS...
I THOUGHT THAT I COULD TAKE IT ALL FOR MYSELF...
BUT I WAS WRONG.
THEY CAPTURED ME IN FAIRY CHAINS.

"Every day I regret what I did," says the dragon. "I now know how wrong I was. But Titania and the fairies have forgotten all about me."

What a sad story! You're glad you didn't listen to Titania and ignore the dragon. After all, you know what it's like to make a bad decision. "Is there any way I could help, dragon?"

The dragon is silent for a minute. "Fairy chains can be broken by spells and riddles," he says finally. "If you answer a riddle correctly, the spell will break. But if you get it wrong, the fairy spell forces me to give you a cruel punishment."

That does sound dangerous. But how hard can a riddle be? "When you're free, can you change me back into a human?"

The dragon bows its head. "You have my word. Here's the riddle:

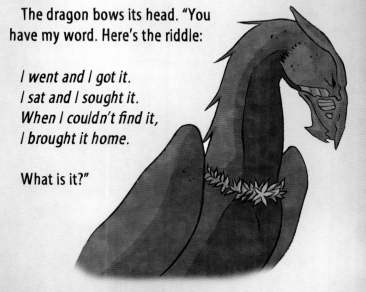

I went and I got it.
I sat and I sought it.
When I couldn't find it,
I brought it home.

What is it?"

GO ON TO THE NEXT PAGE.

Oh no! This one is really tricky. And it sounds like you won't like what happens if you get it wrong.

WILL YOU...

. . . guess "a splinter." That makes sense.
TURN TO PAGE 110.

. . . guess "a fairy curse." You are in Tir na nOg, after all.
TURN TO PAGE 73.

You take a deep breath. "I name you: Kelpie, Finman, and selkie Abby Fraser!" you shout.

For less than a second, the three of them turn to stare at you. They look horrified, and you don't understand. Shouldn't naming them all have saved the Finman and Ms. Fraser from the Kelpie? The three of them groan and then dissolve right before your eyes into a pile of silver coins. One moment they were as real as the wooden spoon in your hand, and the next . . .

You look down and see that the silver coin that fell from your pocket is just one of hundreds on the sea floor. You could be rich, but you leave the silver and swim away.

They're gone, and it's all your fault.

THE END

You try to rip apart the seaweed trapping Ms. Fraser in the lair, but she begs you to leave. You pull the silver fairy coin from your pocket and stand up.

"You must take me to the surface," you say, with far more bravery than you feel.

The Kelpie looks at the coin then snaps its teeth an inch away from your face.

"I like your eyes," it says. "I'm sure they'll be delicious."

But it doesn't eat you, and you cautiously grab its thick tail. With a low-pitched neigh, the water-horse pulls you back through the sea and to the beach.

"My payment!" demands the Kelpie. You toss the coin deep into the water, and he dives to get it, vanishing under the waves.

You never see the Kelpie or Ms. Fraser again. Did she escape? For the rest of your life, whenever you see a seal, you wonder.

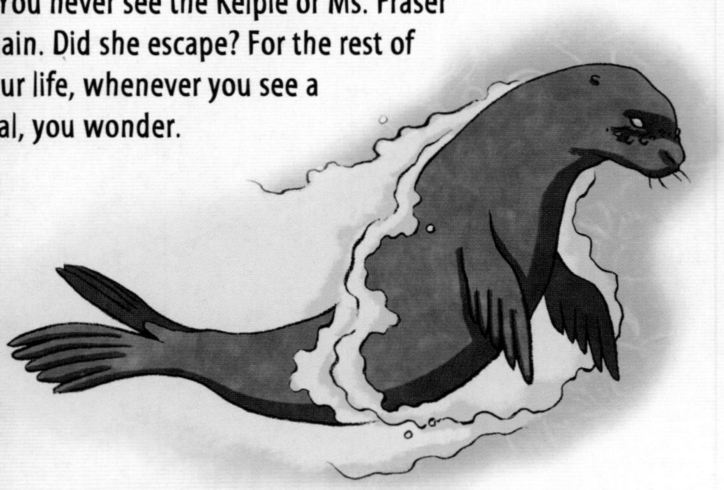

THE END

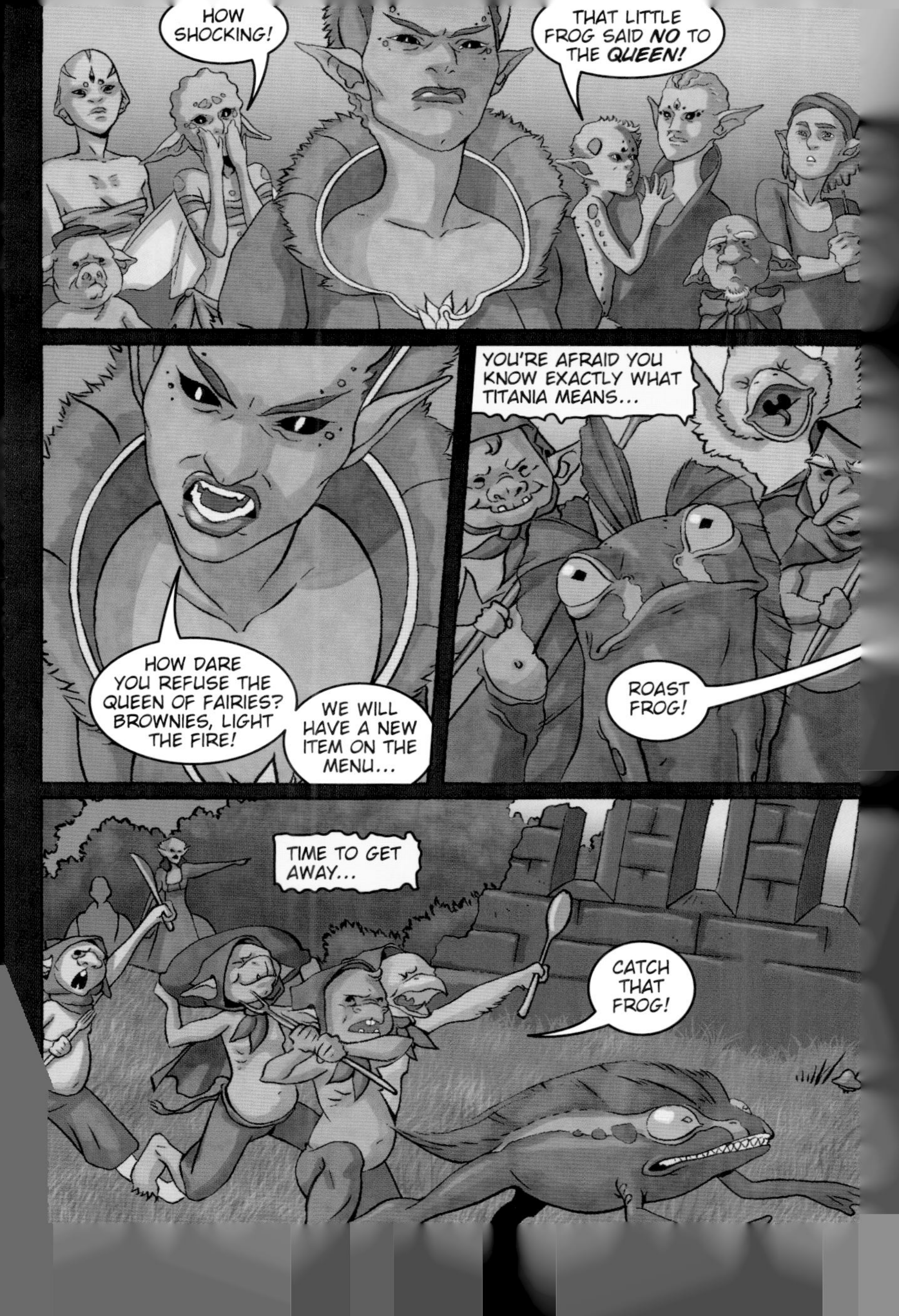
HOW SHOCKING!
THAT LITTLE FROG SAID NO TO THE QUEEN!
HOW DARE YOU REFUSE THE QUEEN OF FAIRIES? BROWNIES, LIGHT THE FIRE!
WE WILL HAVE A NEW ITEM ON THE MENU...
YOU'RE AFRAID YOU KNOW EXACTLY WHAT TITANIA MEANS...
ROAST FROG!
TIME TO GET AWAY...
CATCH THAT FROG!

You jump over the wall of the fairy court just in time. Queen Titania and the other fairies scream behind you, but they don't follow you over the wall. You hop away as fast as your froggy feet can go, until the only sounds you hear are owls and crickets.

Whew. That was close.
You look around and see a
dirt path that stretches on
either side of you. There's
a sudden noise behind
you. You turn and see one
of the brownies from the
fairy court. Should you
run away?

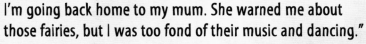

"Wait!" the brownie
calls. "I won't hurt you.
I'm going back home to my mum. She warned me about those fairies, but I was too fond of their music and dancing."

"They're horrible!" you say. "I hope they lose the battle."

"Do you? Then maybe you should join the Goblin King, Robin Goodfellow."

"Could he change me back?"

"Maybe, maybe not. But you're better off with him than the high-and-mighty fairies."

The fairies *are* awful.
But is this Robin Goodfellow any better?

WILL YOU...

...ask the brownie how to find Robin
Goodfellow and the goblins?
TURN TO PAGE 91.

...try to find help on your own?
TURN TO PAGE 14.

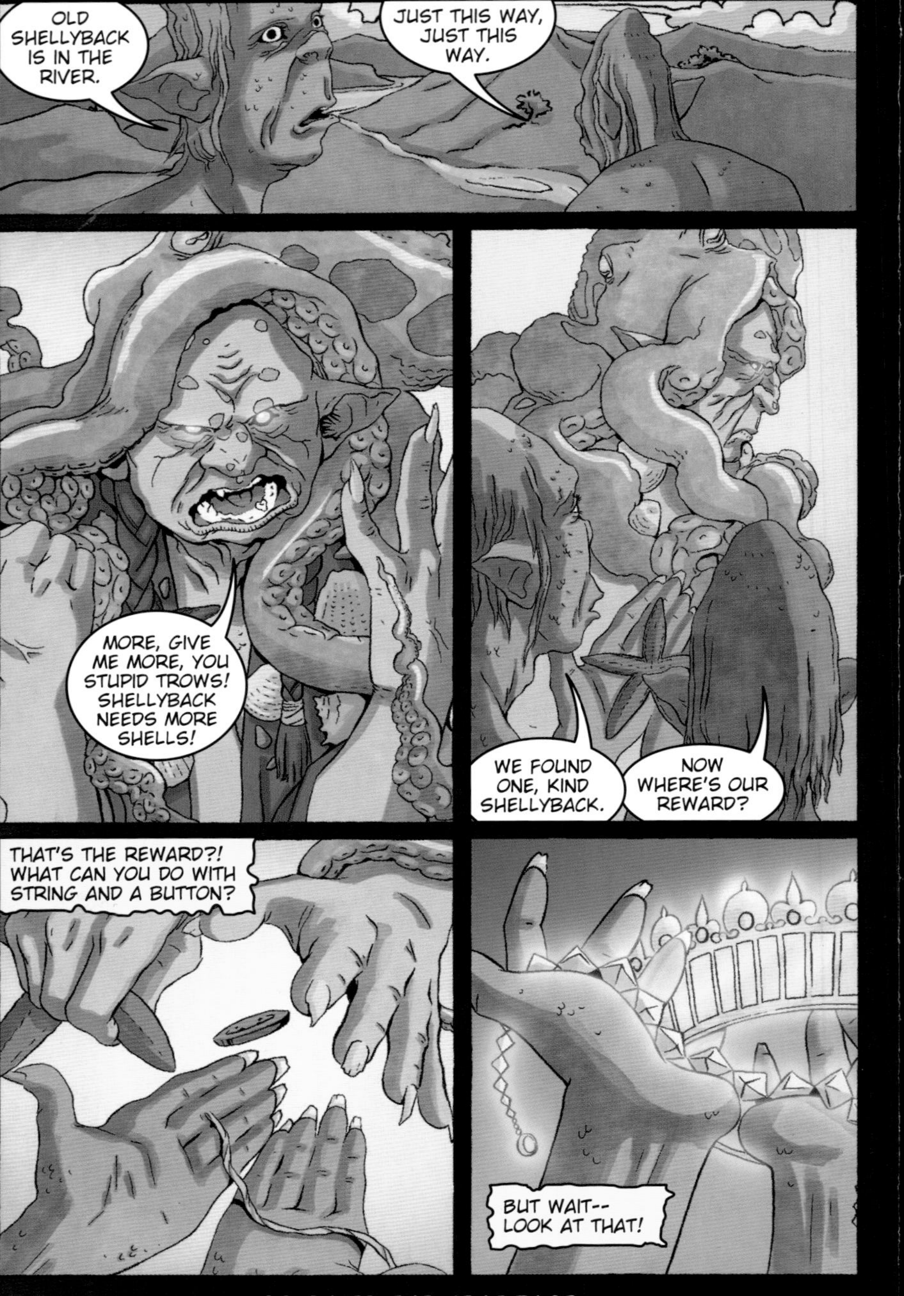
OLD SHELLYBACK IS IN THE RIVER.
JUST THIS WAY, JUST THIS WAY.
MORE, GIVE ME MORE, YOU STUPID TROWS! SHELLYBACK NEEDS MORE SHELLS!
WE FOUND ONE, KIND SHELLYBACK.
NOW WHERE'S OUR REWARD?
THAT'S THE REWARD?! WHAT CAN YOU DO WITH STRING AND A BUTTON?
BUT WAIT-- LOOK AT THAT!

GO ON TO THE NEXT PAGE.

It looks like the Shellyback's rewards aren't so bad. Maybe he'll have something that will help Ms. Fraser after all. You shrug and try your luck searching for shells.

The sea trows may not be the smartest kids in class, but they're way better than you at finding shells. Every time you think you see one under the water, a knobby sea-trow hand snatches it. Frustrated, you move away a few feet. Suddenly, something catches your eye.

"Oh, a glinty one!" says Cob. Quickly, you snatch the object from the water. It's a silver shell in the shape of a horn.

"A sea horn!" says Mog. "Shellyback will give a big reward. He hates Kelpie, he does."

Now you're curious. "What does the sea horn have to do with the Kelpie?"

Mog's big eyes widen. "Oh, Kelpie hates the sound of it. He freezes right up, he does. Can't eat a thing."

You look back at your discovery. This could be useful.

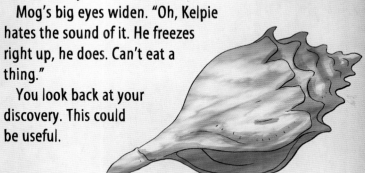

GO ON TO THE NEXT PAGE.

If you use the sea horn, you might be able to save Ms. Fraser from the Kelpie. But if you give it to the Shellyback, he might give you a great reward.

WILL YOU...

...give in to curiosity and get the Shellyback's reward?

TURN TO PAGE 82.

...take the high road and try to save Ms. Fraser?

TURN TO PAGE 50.

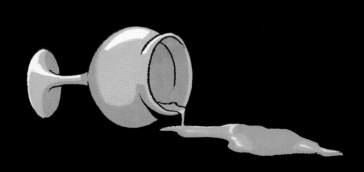

You grip your thistle-sword and hunt through the battle for the frog. There was something so *familiar* in its eyes that you can't just let it go. Suddenly, Oberon's voice stops you in midstep.

"What are you doing here? You should be with Puck at the head of the battle!"

You look up at the tall fairy king. He doesn't seem much like your father.

"Sorry," you mumble, "I saw a frog . . ." And you don't really want to be at the head of the battle anyway.

The king looks stern. "Come!" he says and grabs your elbow. In the corner of your eye, you see a flash of something large and green. You wiggle out of the king's grasp and sprint toward it. "Wait!" you yell. It's heading for the hill above the battlefield.

GO ON TO THE NEXT PAGE.

You really want to find that frog.

WILL YOU...

... go after the green thing by the hill?
It looks a little big, but it's hard to
tell in the confusion of battle.
TURN TO PAGE 47.

... look elsewhere for the frog?
TURN TO PAGE 55

The lady with the gold hair has a very kind smile, and you decide to trust her.

"You'll regret this," says the dark-haired woman.

You hop inside the fairy ring. When the baby sees you, it stops wailing. You scoop it up with your mouth and hop back outside the circle of mushrooms. As soon as the golden-haired lady takes the baby, they both begin to change. The lady shrinks, and the baby grows until two goblins covered with golden fur are grinning at you.

"We're *gruagach*," announces the goblin who used to be a baby. "I was a changeling child—I switched places with a human baby. But the farmer's wife knew better than to keep me in the house, so she put me in a fairy ring that only a human could cross."

The two gruagach move closer to you. "But I'm a mite hungry after all that wailing . . ."

What large teeth they have!

"I told you so," says the dark-haired lady.

And that's the last thing you hear before . . .

THE END

"I think I'd rather dance," you say to Robin Goodfellow. He frowns then claps his hands. The music grows louder until you can barely hear your own thoughts. The hobgoblins and goblins lift you from the ground and carry you into the center of the dancing crowd. They twirl you above their heads and swing you by your froggy arms. At first, you laugh. Then Robin Goodfellow plays his pipes. The goblins dance so fast that you can't breathe.

You try to tell them to stop, but they don't hear you. You start to hop and dance on your own, until you move even faster than the goblins. You're tired, but you can't slow down.

"You want to dance?" says Robin Goodfellow. "Then dance!"

You'll never escape. The goblins have you, and you'll dance for them . . . forever.

THE END

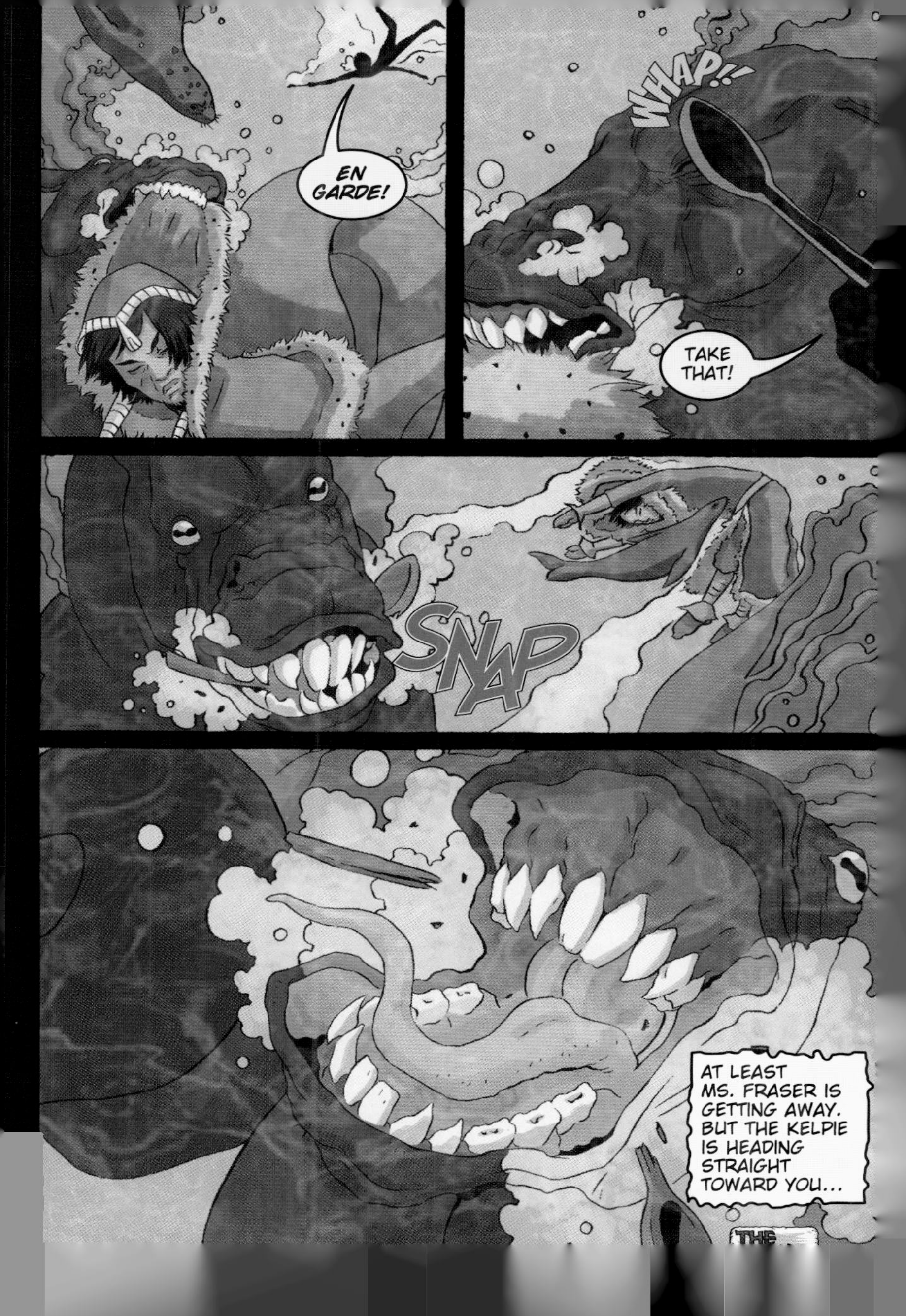
EN GARDE!
WHAP!!
TAKE THAT!
SNAP
AT LEAST MS. FRASER IS GETTING AWAY. BUT THE KELPIE IS HEADING STRAIGHT TOWARD YOU...
THE

The banshee sits atop her pile of bones, combing her long, green hair. She sings a song to herself that sounds like a thousand babies wailing. The banshee pauses as you approach her throne. Her eyes are the color of pond water, and you try not to look at them.

"Why are you here, frog?" asks the banshee. Her voice is the saddest thing you've ever heard.

"I need the Ever-Blooming Branch for Queen Titania."

The banshee seems to understand your ribbits and croaks. "Do you? And why should I let you have it?"

Uh-oh. You try to think of a good answer, but it's hard to be clever when you're staring at a pile of bones.

"Um . . . please?"

You brace yourself for a horrible fate. Instead, the banshee shrugs.

"If you want it, you can go through the door. It's not mine anymore."

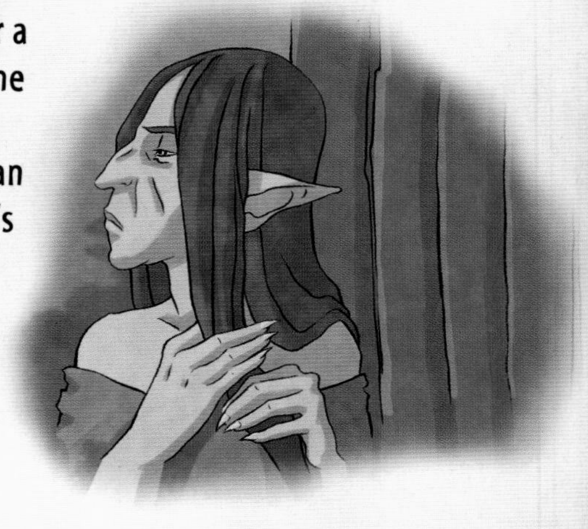

TURN TO PAGE 92.

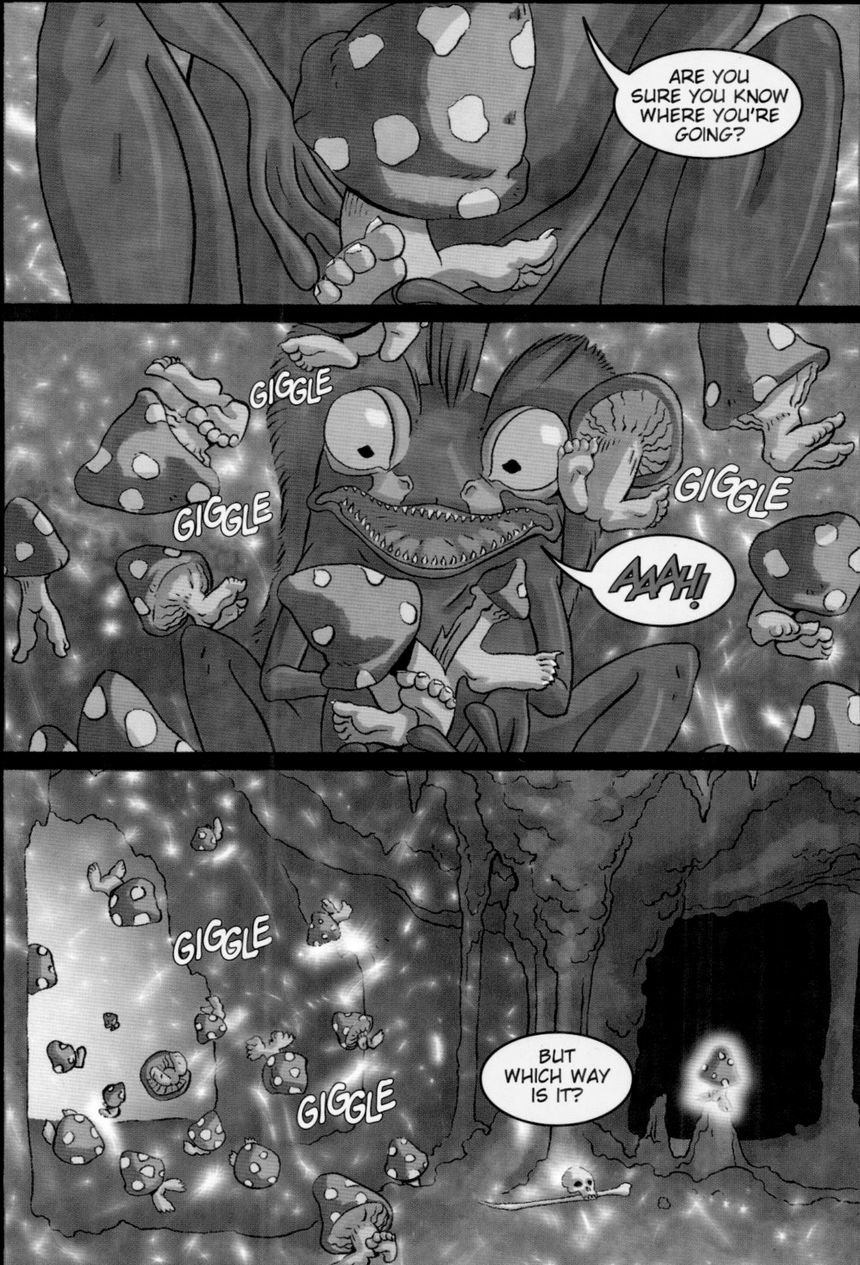
ARE YOU SURE YOU KNOW WHERE YOU'RE GOING?
GIGGLE
GIGGLE
GIGGLE
AAAH!
GIGGLE
GIGGLE
BUT WHICH WAY IS IT?

GO ON TO THE NEXT PAGE.

Now you're definitely lost.
WILL YOU...

...go down the tunnel with most of the mushrooms? There's safety in numbers.
TURN TO PAGE 21.

...trust that the lonely mushroom knows the way?
TURN TO PAGE 74.

You run to Ms. Fraser's room and knock on the door. She opens it, dressed in a long flannel nightgown. You explain to her about the strange voice outside and the woman in the fairy ring.

"Oh my," she says. "Let's have a look."

You follow her down the stairs, but when she opens the door, the fairy is gone!

"It's okay," she says. "The fair folk are tricksy sometimes. Why don't we get you a drink of milk?"

The kitchen is dark, but you hear something humming and scraping inside. Ms. Fraser looks worried and turns on the light. A strange little elf is mixing batter in a bowl!

"Oh, it's just a brownie," Ms. Fraser says. "Have you heard something outside, brownie?"

The little elf frowns. "The sea folk are calling back one of their own. As you well know, Abby Fraser."

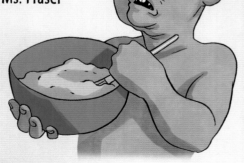

To your surprise, Ms. Fraser blushes.

GO ON TO THE NEXT PAGE.

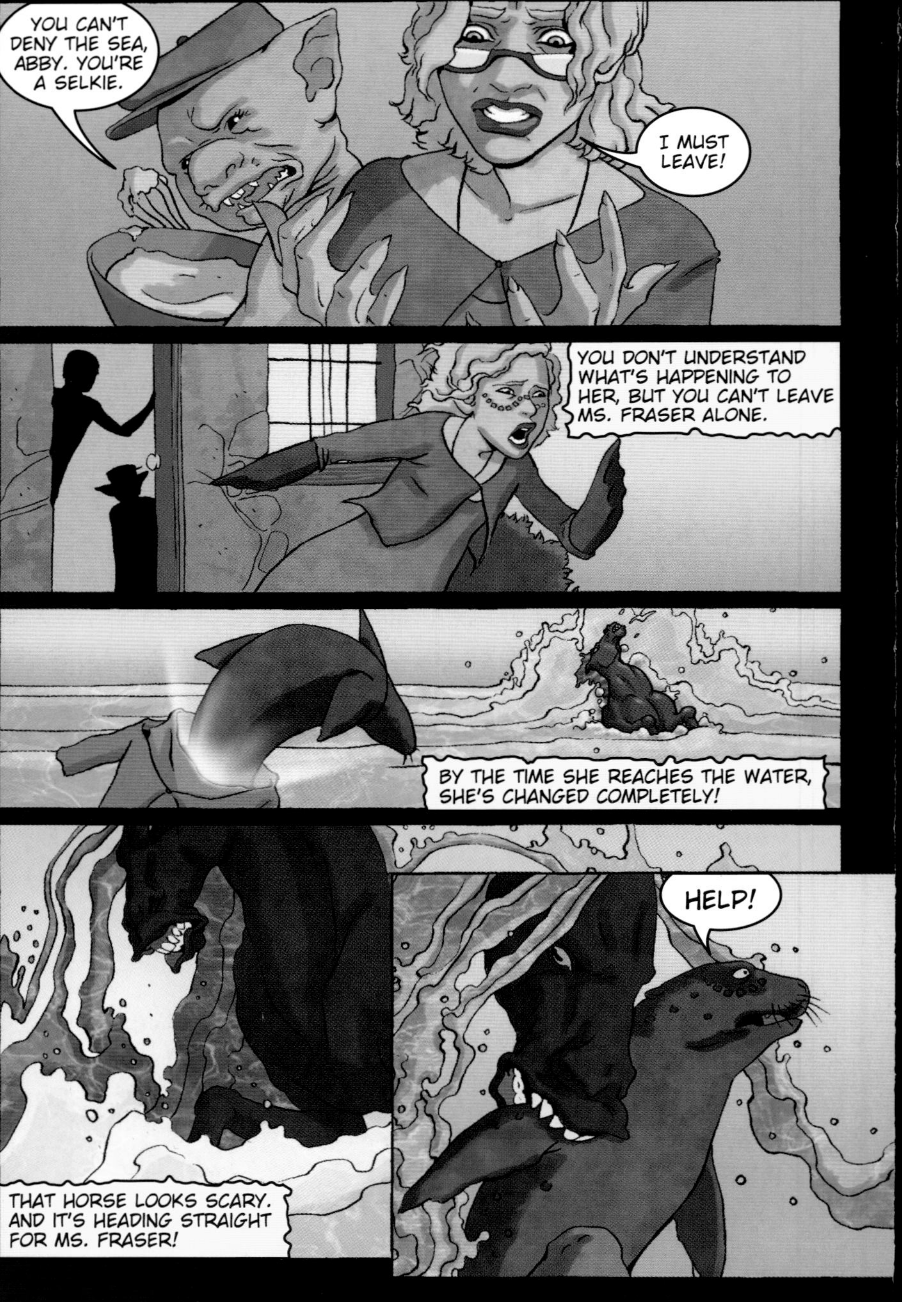
YOU CAN'T DENY THE SEA, ABBY. YOU'RE A SELKIE.
I MUST LEAVE!
YOU DON'T UNDERSTAND WHAT'S HAPPENING TO HER, BUT YOU CAN'T LEAVE MS. FRASER ALONE.
BY THE TIME SHE REACHES THE WATER, SHE'S CHANGED COMPLETELY!
THAT HORSE LOOKS SCARY. AND IT'S HEADING STRAIGHT FOR MS. FRASER!
HELP!

TURN TO PAGE 100.

You don't have the courage to fight Puck, so you just watch in horror as Robin Goodfellow is strangled by the magical vines. The goblins around you try to save their king, but the vines kill anyone who comes too close. Afraid, you hop away. Maybe you should go back to the cave and hide there until it's all over. Suddenly, a voice that sounds like the earth itself booms over the plain.

"What do you bid me do, Puck?" asks the Green Man.

Puck stands beside Robin Goodfellow's body. "Destroy the goblin army," he replies.

The grass beneath your feet ties you and the goblins to the earth. The fairies laugh as they run among you. The last thing you see is Puck's face before a spear of thistle pierces your heart.

THE END

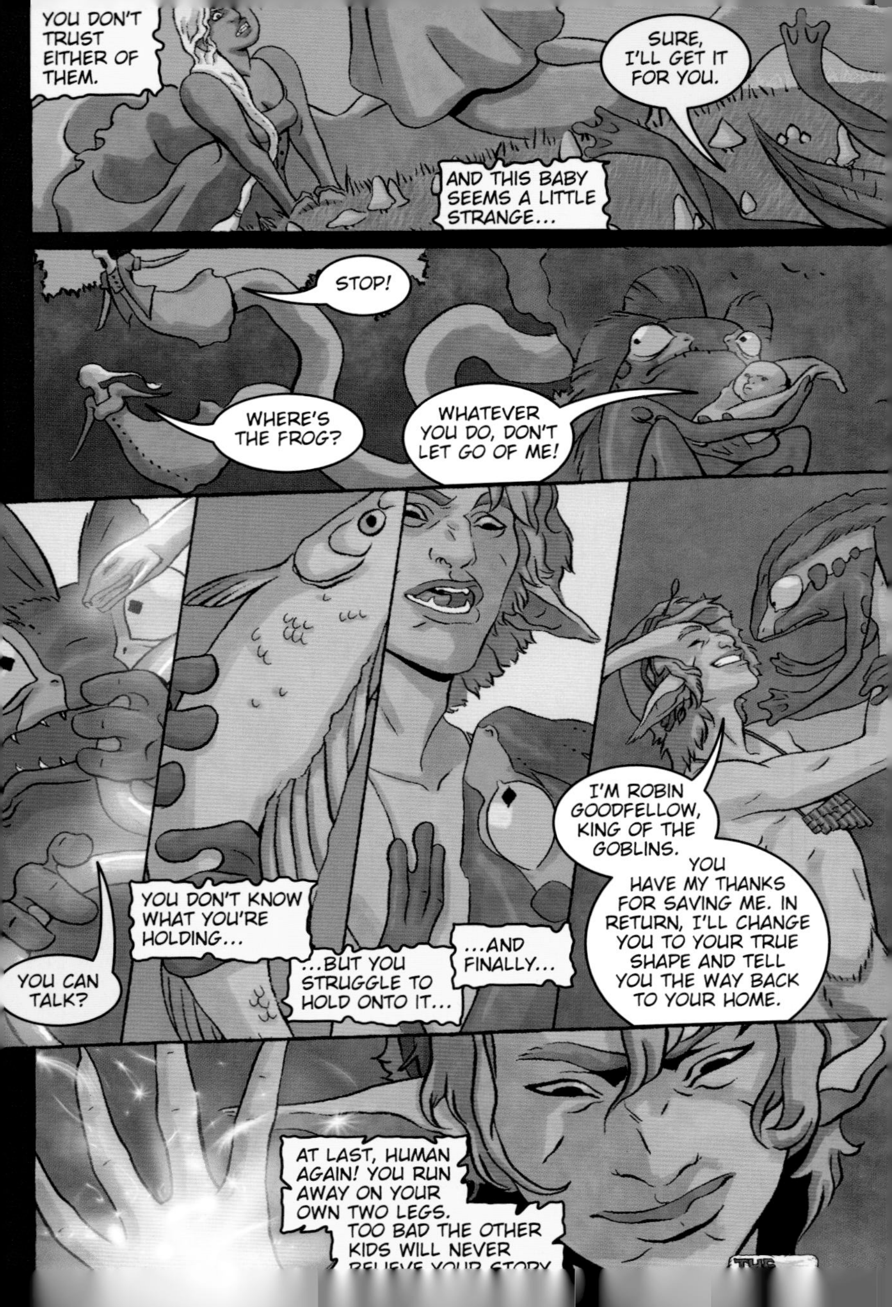
YOU DON'T TRUST EITHER OF THEM.
SURE, I'LL GET IT FOR YOU.
AND THIS BABY SEEMS A LITTLE STRANGE…
STOP!
WHERE'S THE FROG?
WHATEVER YOU DO, DON'T LET GO OF ME!
YOU CAN TALK?
YOU DON'T KNOW WHAT YOU'RE HOLDING…
…BUT YOU STRUGGLE TO HOLD ONTO IT…
…AND FINALLY…
I'M ROBIN GOODFELLOW, KING OF THE GOBLINS.
YOU HAVE MY THANKS FOR SAVING ME. IN RETURN, I'LL CHANGE YOU TO YOUR TRUE SHAPE AND TELL YOU THE WAY BACK TO YOUR HOME.
AT LAST, HUMAN AGAIN! YOU RUN AWAY ON YOUR OWN TWO LEGS.
TOO BAD THE OTHER KIDS WILL NEVER

The Finman's eyes follow the piece of silver as it arcs down to the bottom of the sea. The Kelpie kicks the Finman with his hooves, but the Finman doesn't budge. What's wrong with him?

"The coin!" shouts Ms. Fraser. "Don't you understand? He can't move when he sees silver!"

You swim down with quick strokes and grab the coin just before it touches the sand. Above you, the Finman can move again. But instead of attacking the Kelpie, he starts to sing. You can't believe it—the Kelpie could kill him at any moment! But at the sound of the Finman's voice, you're suddenly surrounded by thousands and thousands of tiny fish and seahorses and starfish. They surround the Kelpie too. Though he bucks, the little animals won't let him go.

"Take him far away," sings the Finman. "Don't let him return."

The Kelpie is lifted in a great cloud of tiny fish and carried away.

GO ON TO THE NEXT PAGE.

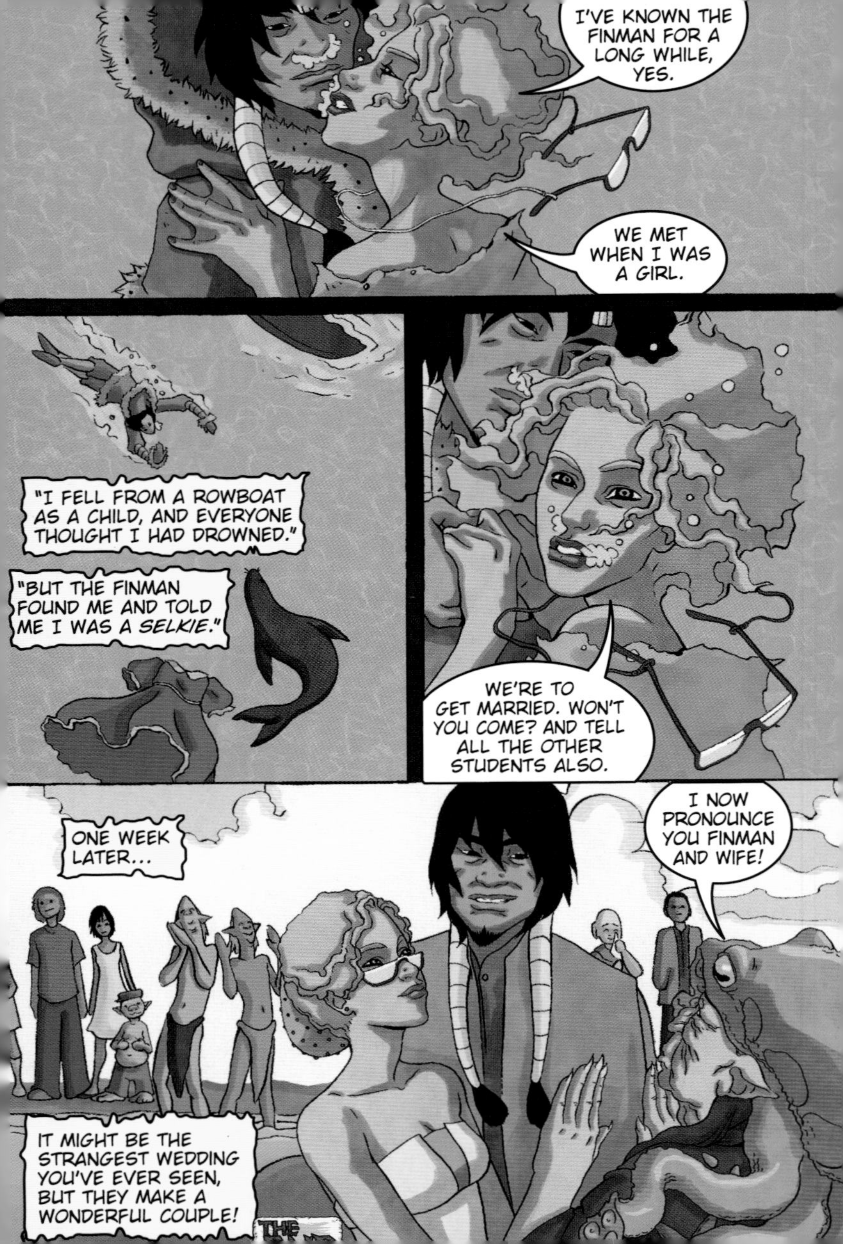
I'VE KNOWN THE FINMAN FOR A LONG WHILE, YES.
WE MET WHEN I WAS A GIRL.
"I FELL FROM A ROWBOAT AS A CHILD, AND EVERYONE THOUGHT I HAD DROWNED."
"BUT THE FINMAN FOUND ME AND TOLD ME I WAS A *SELKIE*."
WE'RE TO GET MARRIED. WON'T YOU COME? AND TELL ALL THE OTHER STUDENTS ALSO.
ONE WEEK LATER...
I NOW PRONOUNCE YOU FINMAN AND WIFE!
IT MIGHT BE THE STRANGEST WEDDING YOU'VE EVER SEEN, BUT THEY MAKE A WONDERFUL COUPLE!
THE

You're panting and sweating by the time you make it to the base of the hill. You look up and see that you weren't chasing the frog at all but the Green Man. The frog is nowhere to be seen.

"What are you doing up here?" you ask the Green Man.

Even though its face is made of twigs and leaves, it seems sad. "Waiting for one side to use me. Then I may be able to leave."

"Why don't you leave now?"

He sighs. "Because they have the branch. Unless . . ."

"What is it?" you ask.

"If a human traveled with me, I might be able to escape. You're from outside of this world. If you tie your fate with mine, the fairies' hold on me might be broken."

You look down at the goblins and fairies fighting below you, and suddenly that seems like a very good idea. You take the Green Man's hand. "Let's leave before they notice."

Slowly, he smiles. Together, you walk away from the battle . . . and, you hope, back toward your own world.

THE END

You run down the stairs and out the front door. The fairy looks like nothing you've ever seen before, with a dress made of cobwebs and butterfly wings and skin that glows blue in the moonlight.

"You are the one who took our coin?" she asks.

Your heart is pounding fast. Since she doesn't seem angry, you nod. "Y-yes. What do you want with me?"

She laughs. It sounds like the wind. "I felt your curiosity from the fairy court itself. You wish to know about us and our world."

You take a deep breath. This is your chance. It's why you answered her call, right? "So, will you take me?" you ask.

She smiles like a cat. You wonder how dangerous she really is. "Take my hand, and I will lead you to Tir na nOg, where all your imaginings are real."

You take her hand and soar into the air.

GO ON TO THE NEXT PAGE.

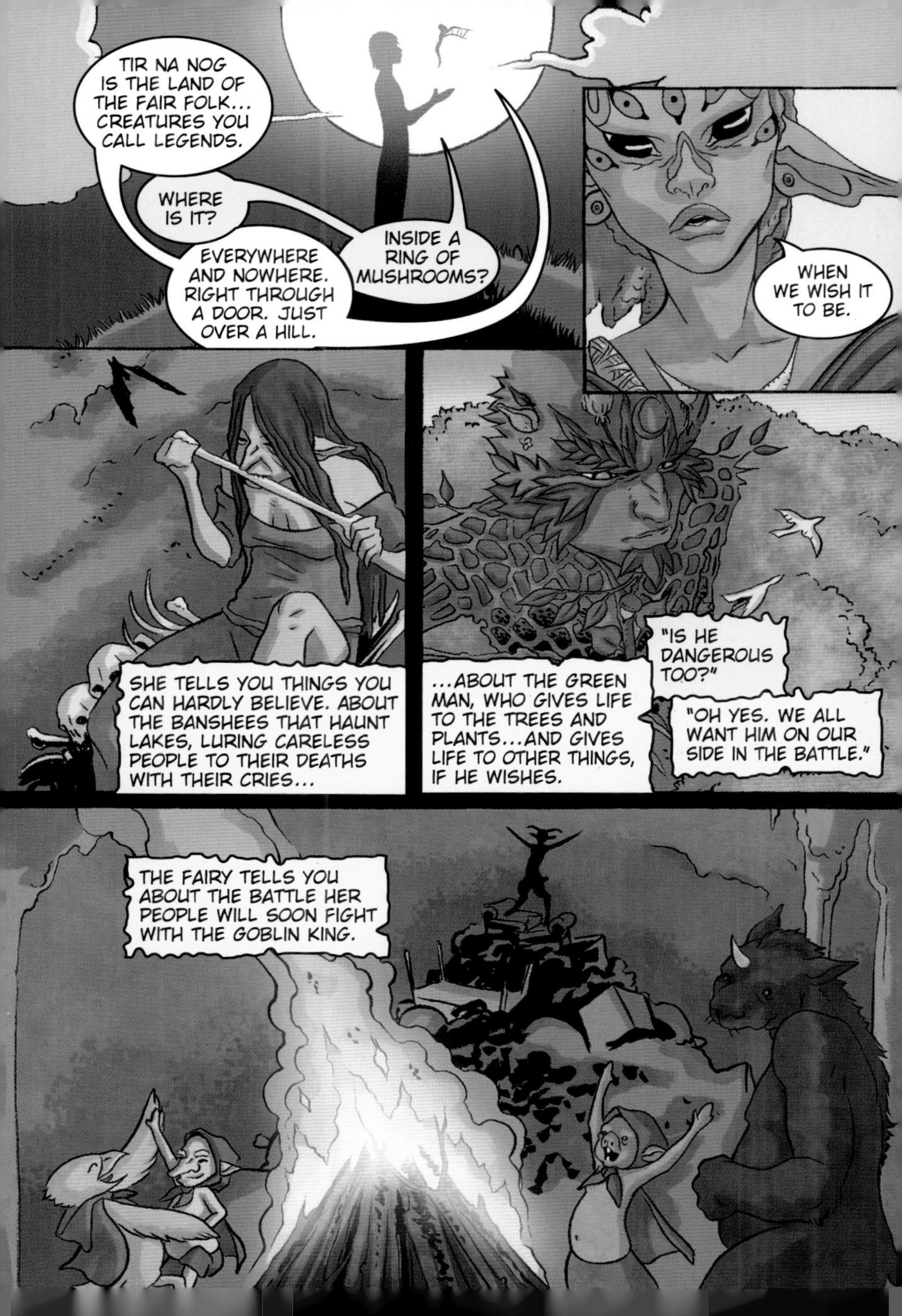
TIR NA NOG IS THE LAND OF THE FAIR FOLK... CREATURES YOU CALL LEGENDS.
WHERE IS IT?
INSIDE A RING OF MUSHROOMS?
EVERYWHERE AND NOWHERE. RIGHT THROUGH A DOOR. JUST OVER A HILL.
WHEN WE WISH IT TO BE.
SHE TELLS YOU THINGS YOU CAN HARDLY BELIEVE. ABOUT THE BANSHEES THAT HAUNT LAKES, LURING CARELESS PEOPLE TO THEIR DEATHS WITH THEIR CRIES...
...ABOUT THE GREEN MAN, WHO GIVES LIFE TO THE TREES AND PLANTS...AND GIVES LIFE TO OTHER THINGS, IF HE WISHES.
"IS HE DANGEROUS TOO?"
"OH YES. WE ALL WANT HIM ON OUR SIDE IN THE BATTLE."
THE FAIRY TELLS YOU ABOUT THE BATTLE HER PEOPLE WILL SOON FIGHT WITH THE GOBLIN KING.

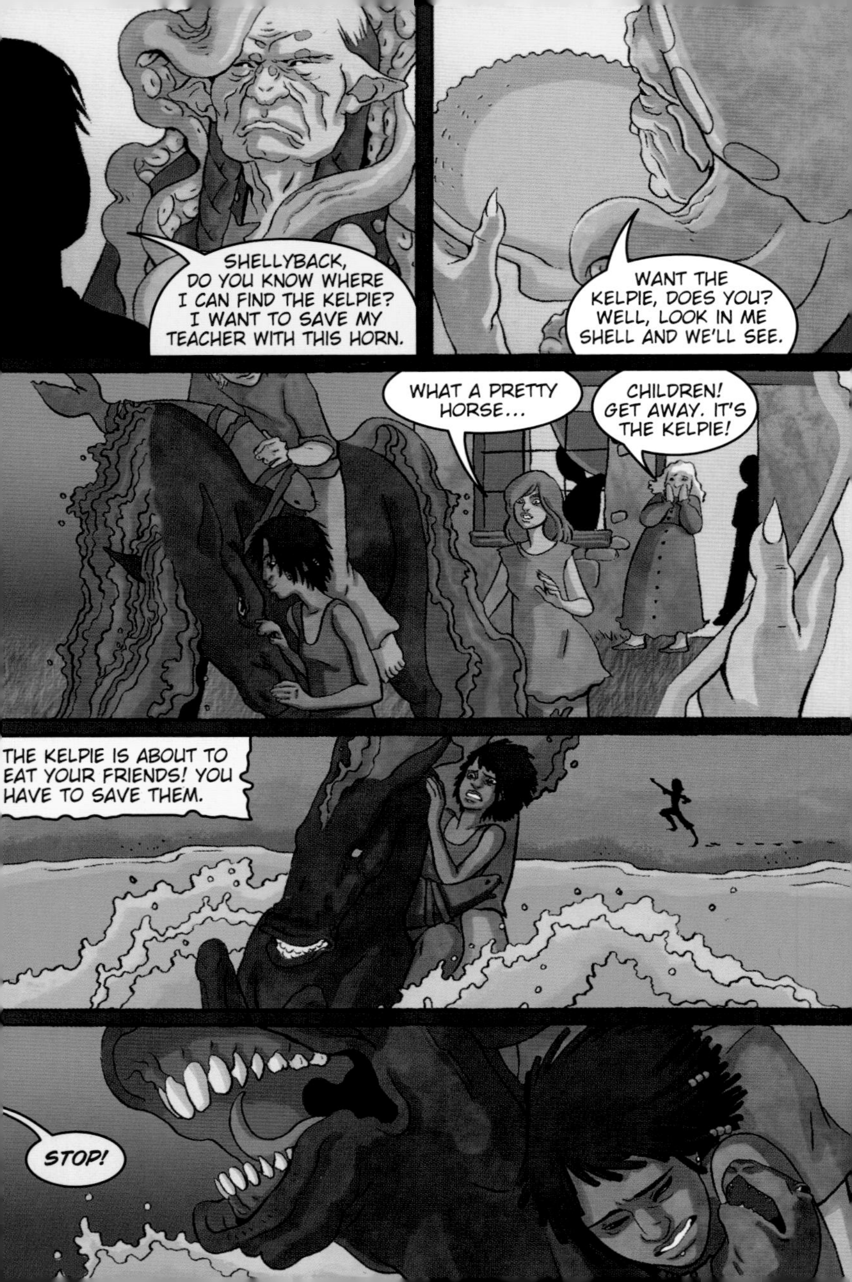

SHELLYBACK, DO YOU KNOW WHERE I CAN FIND THE KELPIE? I WANT TO SAVE MY TEACHER WITH THIS HORN.
WANT THE KELPIE, DOES YOU? WELL, LOOK IN ME SHELL AND WE'LL SEE.
WHAT A PRETTY HORSE...
CHILDREN! GET AWAY. IT'S THE KELPIE!
THE KELPIE IS ABOUT TO EAT YOUR FRIENDS! YOU HAVE TO SAVE THEM.
STOP!

You take a quick step back from the fairy. "No thanks," you say. You're not sure what's in the goblet, but it's better to be safe. The male fairy laughs and bows deeply before you.

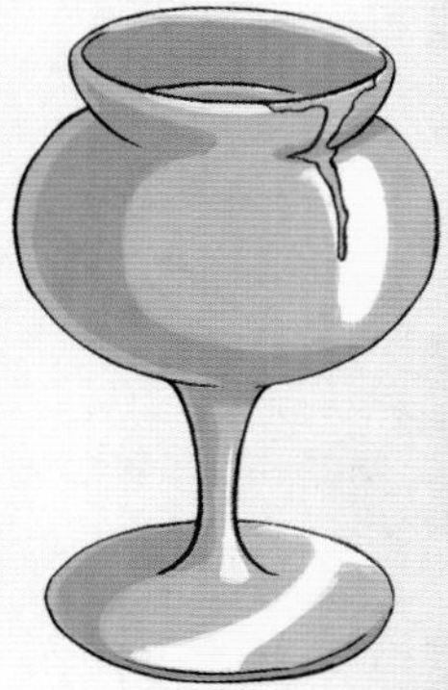

"Your majesties!" he shouts above the music. "Your child has returned and has chosen well!"

The fairies in the room erupt in applause. Queen Titania and King Oberon walk toward you.

Queen Titania smiles. "You have proven yourself worthy, my changeling child."

"*Your*—?" Nothing they're saying makes sense. "What's a changeling child?"

"Years ago, a hobgoblin took you from us and switched you with a real human child."

"We have been searching for you all this time," says Oberon.

You can't believe what you're hearing. *You're* a fairy? "Why would the hobgoblin do that?" you ask.

Queen Titania smashes her scepter to the ground angrily. "Because he hates our power. He calls himself the Goblin King, and tonight we battle against him."

GO ON TO THE NEXT PAGE.

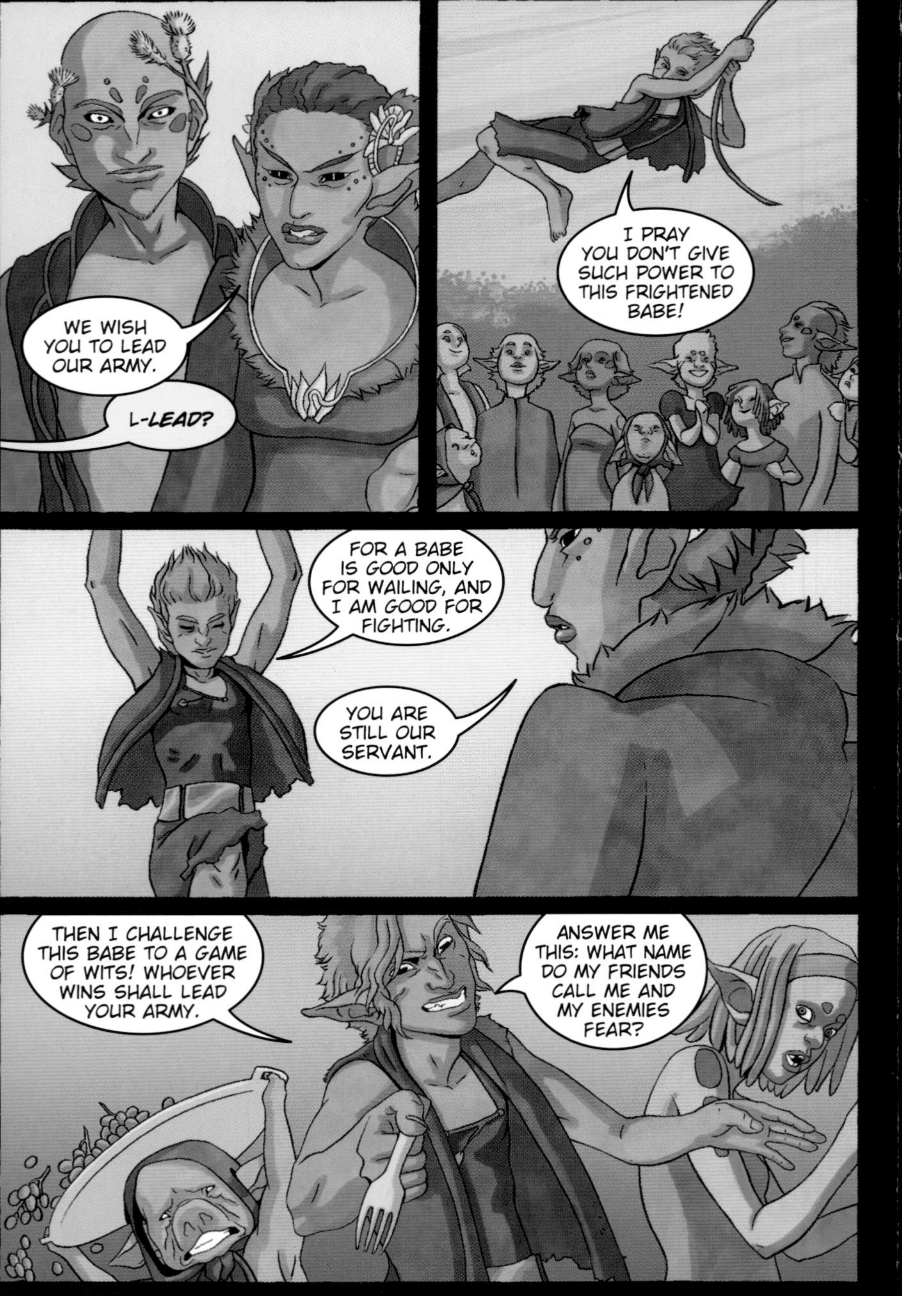
WE WISH YOU TO LEAD OUR ARMY.
L-LEAD?
I PRAY YOU DON'T GIVE SUCH POWER TO THIS FRIGHTENED BABE!
FOR A BABE IS GOOD ONLY FOR WAILING, AND I AM GOOD FOR FIGHTING.
YOU ARE STILL OUR SERVANT.
THEN I CHALLENGE THIS BABE TO A GAME OF WITS! WHOEVER WINS SHALL LEAD YOUR ARMY.
ANSWER ME THIS: WHAT NAME DO MY FRIENDS CALL ME AND MY ENEMIES FEAR?

TURN TO PAGE 81.

The dark-haired one seems like she would be able to help you.

"What will you do to the baby?" you ask.

"Put a leash on it, of course. It's much too dangerous to be left to wail on the moors."

It doesn't look dangerous, but you know you can't trust your eyes in Tir na nOg. The baby screams when you pick it up and give it to her. You wish you could put your hands over your ears.

"I confine you to your natural shape!" says the dark-haired lady. Before your eyes, the baby grows and changes into a huge wolf with red eyes and gray fur. It tries to get away from the dark-haired lady, but there is a leash of fire around its throat.

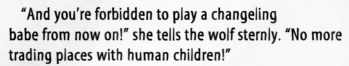

"And you're forbidden to play a changeling babe from now on!" she tells the wolf sternly. "No more trading places with human children!"

GO ON TO THE NEXT PAGE.

The golden-haired lady pouts. "You *know* it was my turn."

"Well, the frog chose me, *sister*."

You stare at the two of them. "You're sisters?"

"Of course," says the dark-haired one. "Look."

She lifts up her skirt, and you gasp. Instead of legs, the two sisters are joined by the same serpent's tail. "We should send you back to your home now, shouldn't we?"

She snaps her fingers, and a great wind lifts you up into the air. You land gently on the doorstep of the inn.

Ms. Fraser is surprised to find you the next morning. Everyone points and takes pictures, but they don't understand your croaks and ribbits. Soon a truck comes, and you're hauled off to the zoo. They give you a big pond and lots of flies to eat, and Ms. Fraser comes by once a week with a treat.

It isn't the life you expected, but you kind of like the flies.

THE END

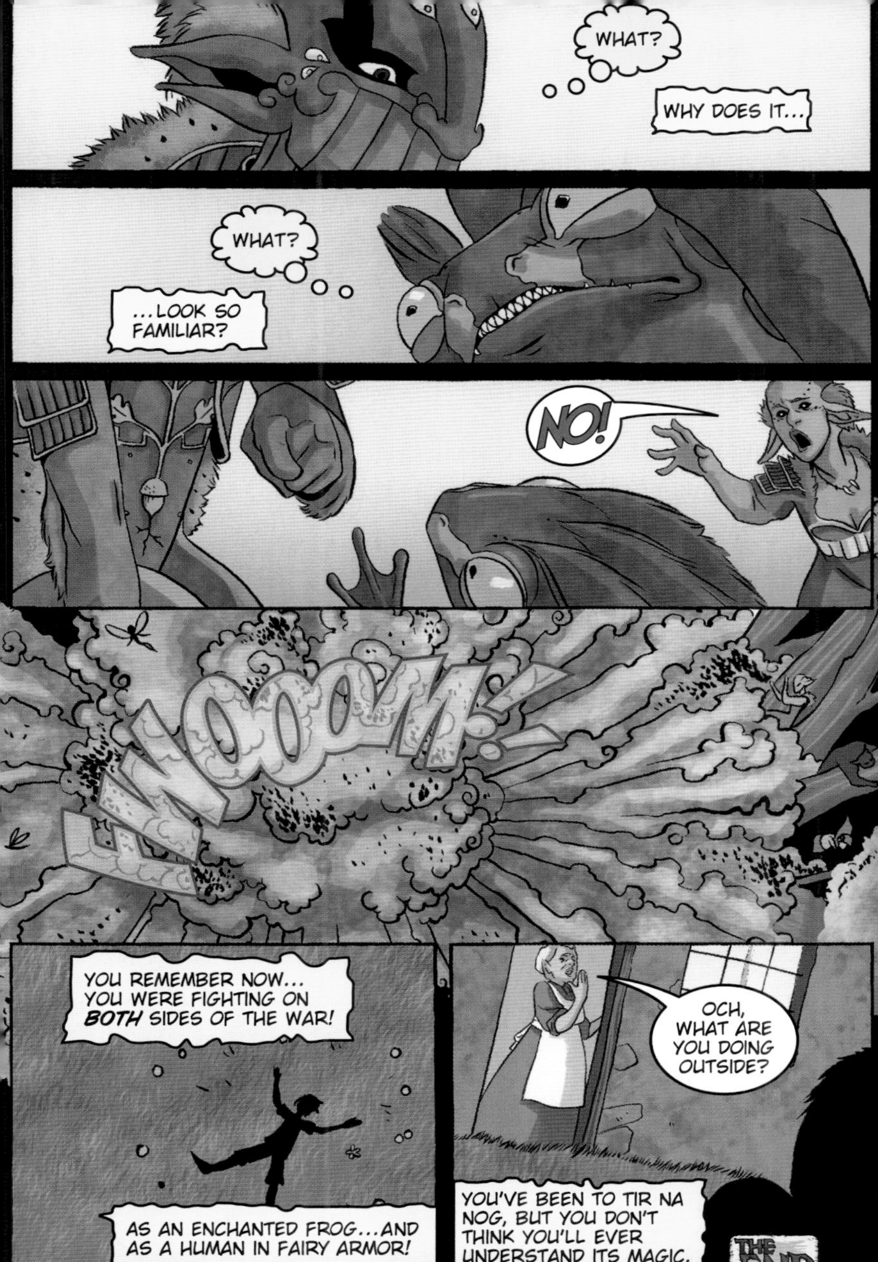
WHAT?
WHY DOES IT...
WHAT?
...LOOK SO FAMILIAR?
NO!
WHOOOM!!
YOU REMEMBER NOW... YOU WERE FIGHTING ON BOTH SIDES OF THE WAR!
AS AN ENCHANTED FROG...AND AS A HUMAN IN FAIRY ARMOR!
OCH, WHAT ARE YOU DOING OUTSIDE?
YOU'VE BEEN TO TIR NA NOG, BUT YOU DON'T THINK YOU'LL EVER UNDERSTAND ITS MAGIC.
THE

You wipe a tear from the corner of your eye. You wish you didn't have to leave. But you can't just abandon your family and everyone else you love. You can't leave everything for a life with creatures you barely understand.

"I'm sorry," you say, "it's just . . ."

The girl puts her finger to your lips. "Shh. We understand," she says. "If you miss us, play your music. We'll be nearby, in every note you play."

"I promise," you say.

The old man embraces you before they leave. You wave until the sun begins to rise, and suddenly, all the fairies disappear.

Years later, people tell you that your music seems to come from another world.

"It does," you always say.

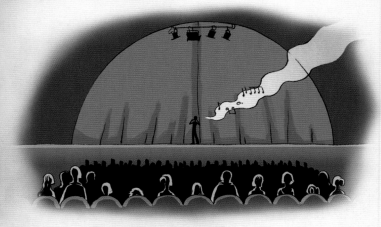

THE END

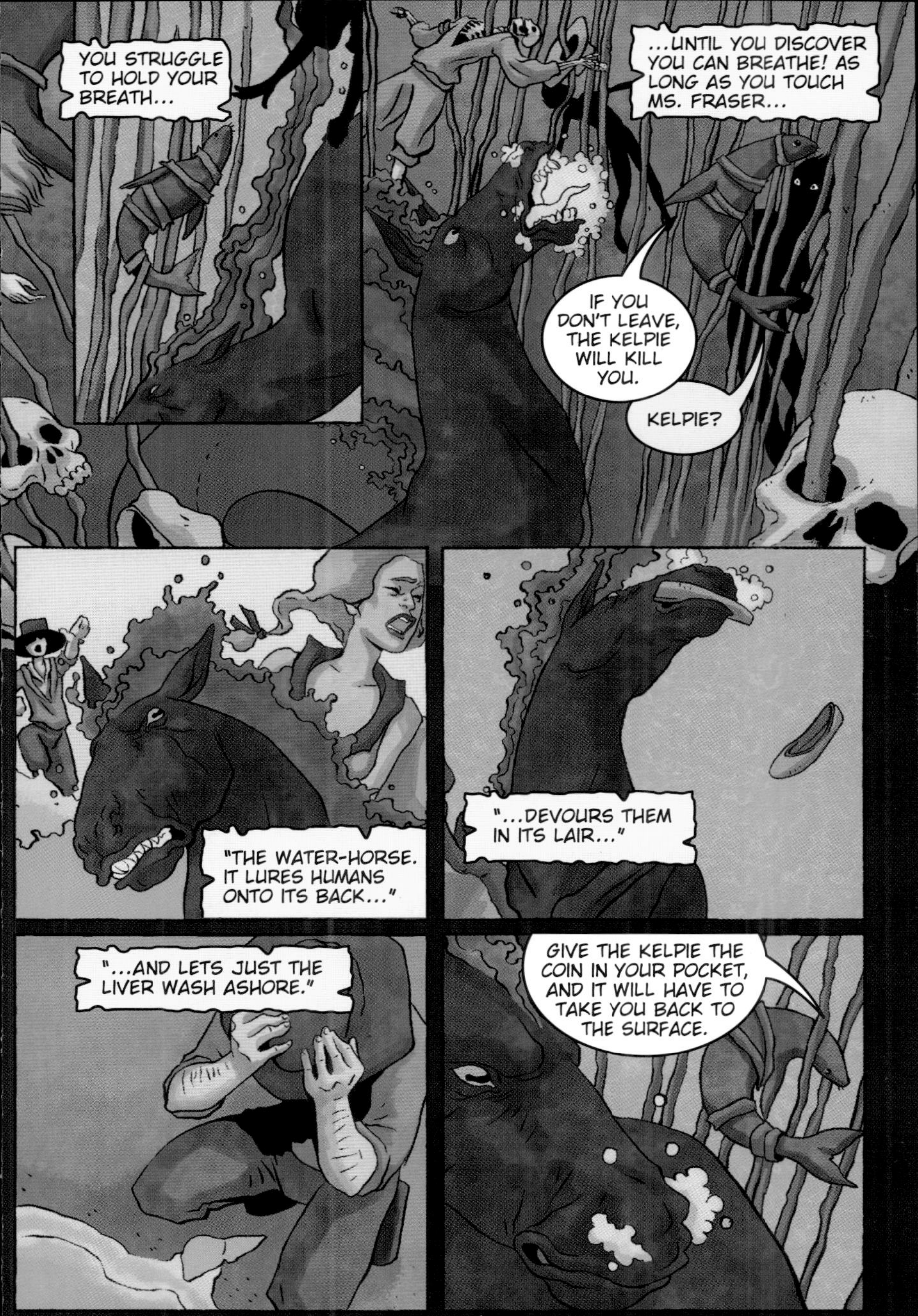
YOU STRUGGLE TO HOLD YOUR BREATH...
...UNTIL YOU DISCOVER YOU CAN BREATHE! AS LONG AS YOU TOUCH MS. FRASER...
IF YOU DON'T LEAVE, THE KELPIE WILL KILL YOU.
KELPIE?
"THE WATER-HORSE. IT LURES HUMANS ONTO ITS BACK..."
"...DEVOURS THEM IN ITS LAIR..."
"...AND LETS JUST THE LIVER WASH ASHORE."
GIVE THE KELPIE THE COIN IN YOUR POCKET, AND IT WILL HAVE TO TAKE YOU BACK TO THE SURFACE.

GO ON TO THE NEXT PAGE.

Ms. Fraser might die if you abandon her now.
And you might die if you stay.
WILL YOU...

. . . heed her advice and give
the coin to the Kelpie?
TURN TO PAGE 26.

. . . stay to help Ms. Fraser?
TURN TO PAGE 89.

You remember a really hard riddle your English teacher once taught you. No one in the class guessed the answer. You bet that Puck won't either.

What can run but never walks,
Has a mouth but never talks,
Has a head but never weeps,
Has a bed but never sleeps?

All the fairies fall silent. You must have stumped him! But the smile freezes on your face. Suddenly, everyone in the room is laughing so hard that tears stream from their eyes.

"Such a child!" laughs Puck.

The queen sighs. "Oh, do what you will with him."

You don't understand what everyone finds so funny. "But you never answered the riddle!"

Puck runs to the table and grabs a skewer of roasted crickets. "A river, of course! Why, we fairies invented that riddle! And now that I have won, you must do as I say." He holds a cricket under your nose. "Open wide."

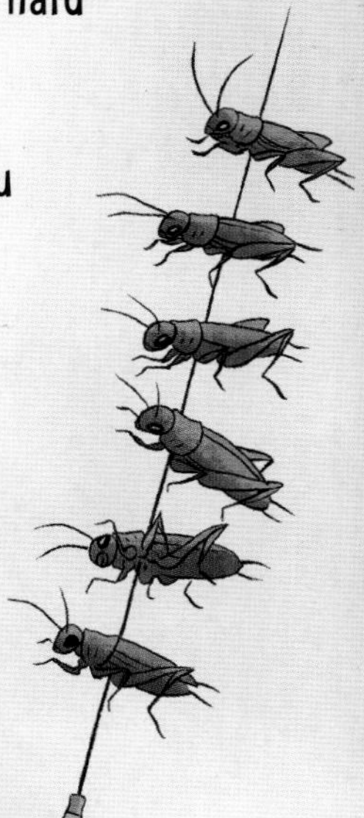

GO ON TO THE NEXT PAGE.

Wait, that isn't fair! You open your mouth to ask the queen for help, and Puck tosses a cricket inside. You grimace, but actually it tastes . . . delicious.

"And it makes the dancing lovely," Puck says. By the time he and most of the fairies leave for battle, it's hard to think. The fairy hall seems to glow more brightly than it did before. For endless hours, you want to do nothing but dance, and you never feel tired or thirsty. What an amazing cricket! At some point in your dance, the other fairies return from battle. You don't ask them who won. Nothing matters to you but the dance. A fairy you recognize, the one who led you to the fairy court, takes your hands and leads you away from the musicians.

"Through the door," she whispers in your ear. You don't want to leave, but she pushes you through the empty stone arch.

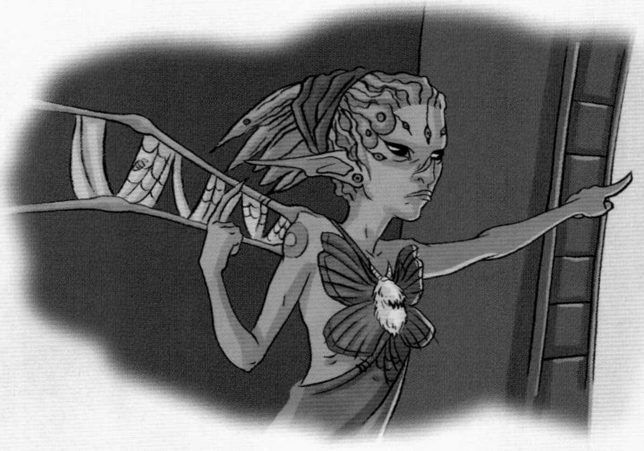

GO ON TO THE NEXT PAGE.

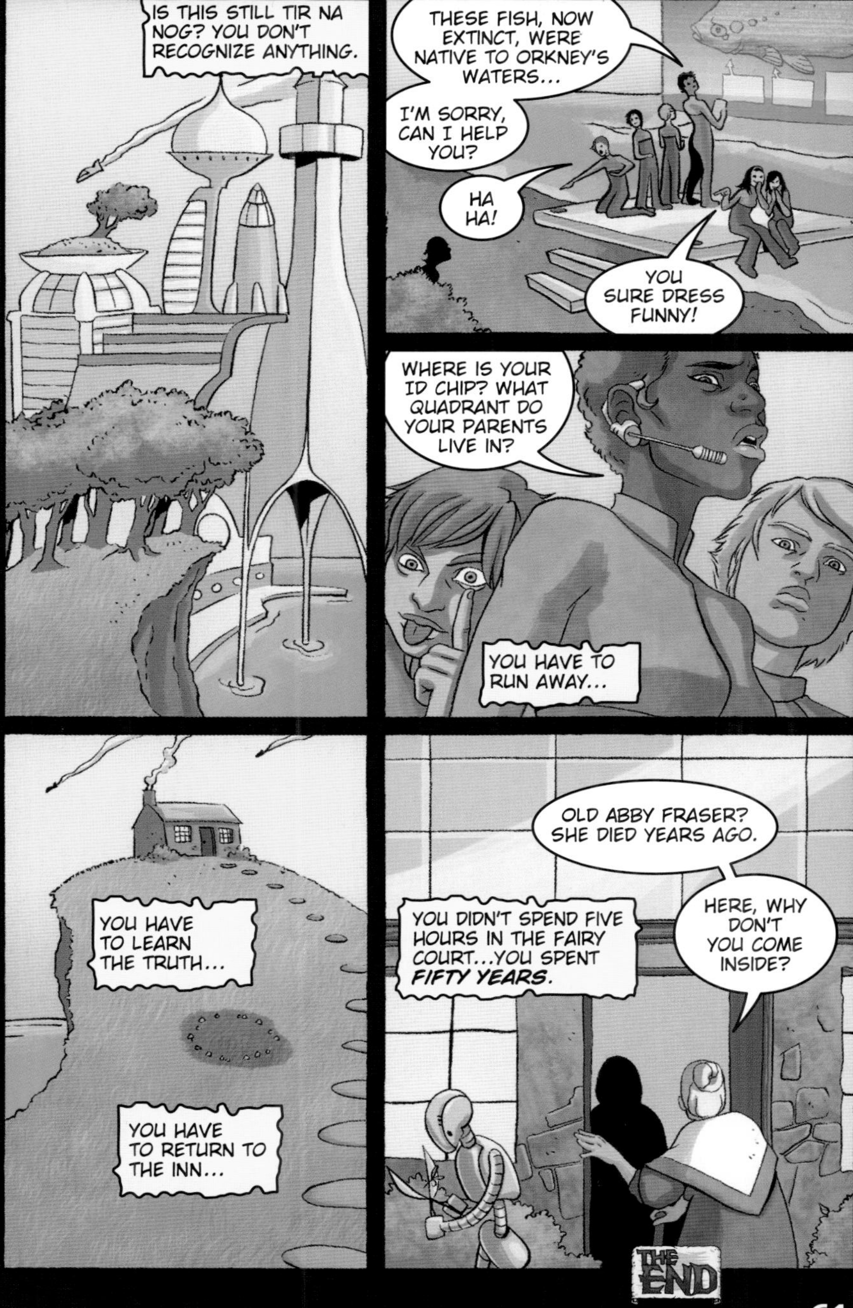
IS THIS STILL TIR NA NOG? YOU DON'T RECOGNIZE ANYTHING.
THESE FISH, NOW EXTINCT, WERE NATIVE TO ORKNEY'S WATERS...
I'M SORRY, CAN I HELP YOU?
HA HA!
YOU SURE DRESS FUNNY!
WHERE IS YOUR ID CHIP? WHAT QUADRANT DO YOUR PARENTS LIVE IN?
YOU HAVE TO RUN AWAY...
YOU HAVE TO LEARN THE TRUTH...
YOU HAVE TO RETURN TO THE INN...
OLD ABBY FRASER? SHE DIED YEARS AGO.
YOU DIDN'T SPEND FIVE HOURS IN THE FAIRY COURT...YOU SPENT ***FIFTY YEARS***.
HERE, WHY DON'T YOU COME INSIDE?
THE END

The goblins seem like a lot more
fun than the fairies.

WILL YOU...

...agree to fight?
TURN TO PAGE 10.

...dance? Around here, a
dancing frog is almost normal.
TURN TO PAGE 36.

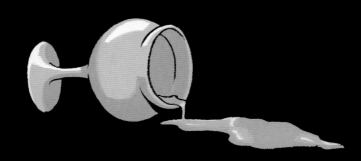

"You can take home all the coins you can swallow," says the little man.

You dip your wet nose to the ground and scoop up a coin. Each piece of silver tastes like the sweetest fruit you've ever eaten. Raspberries, plums, oranges, pineapples, grapes, and melons slide down your throat. The coins start to feel as heavy as a stone in your belly, but you still want more. You gulp another coin near the little man's feet. It tastes like honeysuckle on a hot summer's day. You look around, but to your surprise, not a single coin remains.

"More!" you croak. You don't want anything but that wonderful taste. You try to move, but the coins in your belly are too heavy.

The little man grins. "Thank you! I was tired of guarding this." He puts the Ever-Blooming Branch in your mouth. "Take good care of it. At least—until the next fool comes along!"

You watch in despair as the little man walks through the door. You're all alone now. And you might be alone forever.

THE END

As fast as you can, you scramble up the hill. The brownie is standing on the doorstep when you make it back to the inn.

"A black horse stole Ms. Fraser!"

The brownie walks toward you. "Stolen by the Kelpie? That's a fierce beast."

"Can you help me save her?"

He shakes his head. "Oh no, not I. But I know someone who can," he says.

Gratefully, you follow the brownie back down to the beach.

"Cob, Mog, your cousin calls!"

The water starts to swirl, and two creatures that look like large monkeys without fur crawl onto the beach.

"These are my cousins, the sea trows," says the brownie. "They can help you."

He hands you the wooden spoon from the kitchen. "If you hold this, you can breathe underwater. Please, save her!"

GO ON TO THE NEXT PAGE.

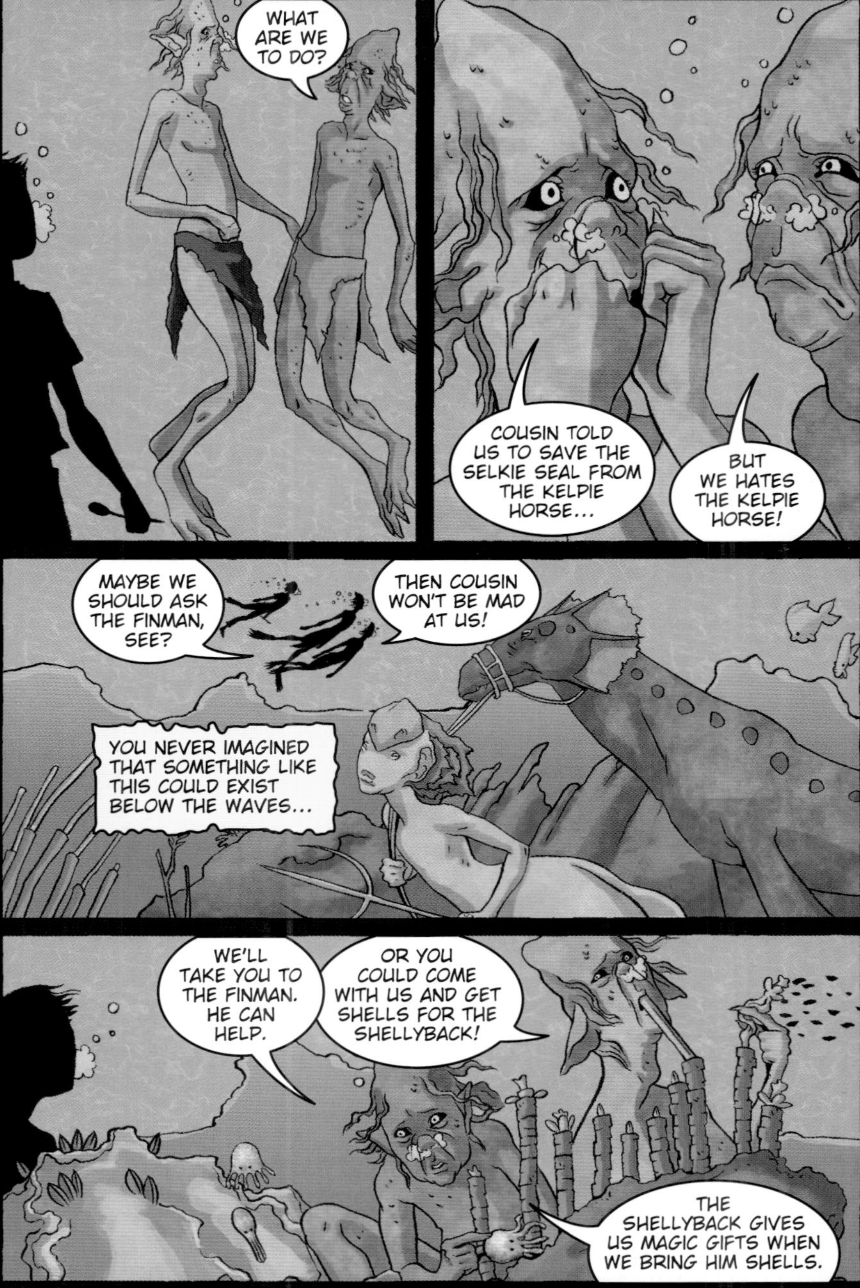
WHAT ARE WE TO DO?
COUSIN TOLD US TO SAVE THE SELKIE SEAL FROM THE KELPIE HORSE...
BUT WE HATES THE KELPIE HORSE!
MAYBE WE SHOULD ASK THE FINMAN, SEE?
THEN COUSIN WON'T BE MAD AT US!
YOU NEVER IMAGINED THAT SOMETHING LIKE THIS COULD EXIST BELOW THE WAVES...
WE'LL TAKE YOU TO THE FINMAN. HE CAN HELP.
OR YOU COULD COME WITH US AND GET SHELLS FOR THE SHELLYBACK!
THE SHELLYBACK GIVES US MAGIC GIFTS WHEN WE BRING HIM SHELLS.

GO ON TO THE NEXT PAGE.

These two sure don't seem that bright.
WILL YOU...

...go off on your own?
Anything would be better than these bozos.
TURN TO PAGE 17.

...trust them and find the Finman
(whoever that is)?
TURN TO PAGE 96.

...go with them to the Shellyback?
Maybe his gifts will be useful.
TURN TO PAGE 30.

You and the other musicians stay on a hill above the fighting on the plain. You have so much fun playing that when the moon finally sinks below the horizon, you're not even sure for a while that the fairy army won.

"Oh, we must be getting back by sunrise," says the old man.

"Yes, you'll never be able to live in Tir na nOg unless you spend a night and a day in our realm," says the girl.

You look down at the pipes in your hand. "If I go back to my world, will I still be able to play music?" you ask.

"Of course," says the old man. "You are your parents' child."

"And if I stay here?"

The old man smiles. "You will be treated as one of our own. You will be royalty in the fairest court in Tir na nOg."

GO ON TO THE NEXT PAGE.

This is your toughest decision yet.
WILL YOU...

...leave the fairies at sunrise?
TURN TO PAGE 56.

...stay with them and become part of the fairy court?
TURN TO PAGE 111.

You jump through the ghosts in front of you and search for a place to hide. You can smell the red cap, even though he's still yards away. He smells like rotting meat and musty clothes. Finally, you see a door at the end of a hallway. You push it open with your nose and hop inside. It's pitch black in here. You hold your breath and strain to hear if the red cap is nearby. Nothing. Your plan worked!

You breathe a sigh of relief. That's when you notice the smell again. It washes over you so strongly it's as though he's standing right outside . . .

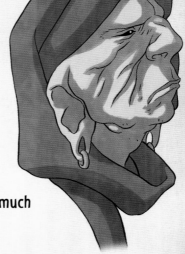

"Ah hah!" he says, throwing open the closet door. "Always trust me nose."

You try to get away, but he lifts his claws to grab your neck.

"Och, I hate froggies," he says.

And by then, of course, it's much too late to run.

THE END

You try to hop away from the laughing fairies, but they won't let you leave. Their laughter hurts your ears, like fingernails on a blackboard.

"Come here, froggie!" one calls.

"Want to dance, froggie?" says another.

Now you know why Ms. Fraser said that fairy feasts are dangerous! If only you hadn't been so thirsty.

Suddenly, a voice rings out from nearby. "What is this?" asks Titania.

The fairies fall silent and move aside for their queen. She regards you seriously. "You wish to be human again?"

"Yes!" you croak. "Won't you turn me back?"

To your surprise, she seems to understand you. "Deep in the earth is a cave guarded by a banshee and a dragon," she says. "The banshee protects the sacred Ever-Blooming Branch. Whoever possesses it will control the Green Man during the goblin battle. Will you get it for us? If you do, I shall give you a reward."

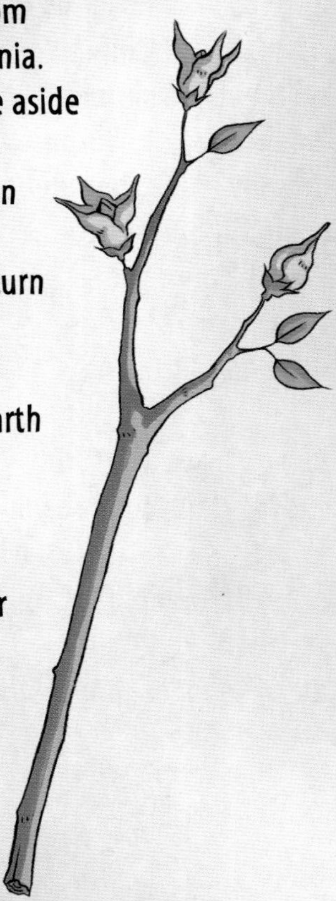

GO ON TO THE NEXT PAGE.

If you get the tree branch, Titania might turn you back to normal. On the other hand, banshees and dragons sound really dangerous. Is it worth it?

WILL YOU...

. . . accept her offer and try to find the magical branch?
TURN TO PAGE 103.

. . . tell her to find someone else for her suicide mission?
TURN TO PAGE 27.

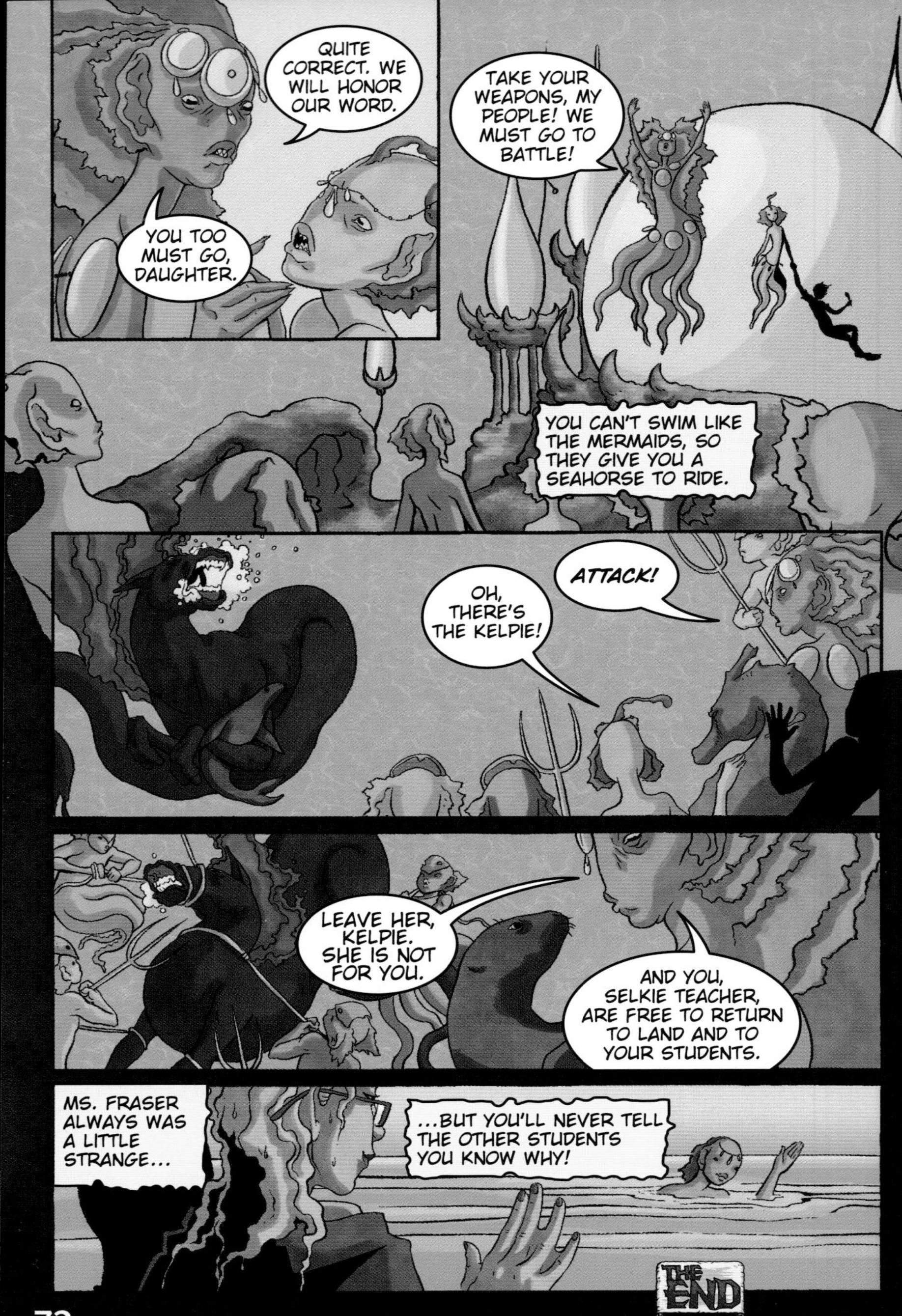
QUITE CORRECT. WE WILL HONOR OUR WORD.
YOU TOO MUST GO, DAUGHTER.
TAKE YOUR WEAPONS, MY PEOPLE! WE MUST GO TO BATTLE!
YOU CAN'T SWIM LIKE THE MERMAIDS, SO THEY GIVE YOU A SEAHORSE TO RIDE.
OH, THERE'S THE KELPIE!
ATTACK!
LEAVE HER, KELPIE. SHE IS NOT FOR YOU.
AND YOU, SELKIE TEACHER, ARE FREE TO RETURN TO LAND AND TO YOUR STUDENTS.
MS. FRASER ALWAYS WAS A LITTLE STRANGE...
...BUT YOU'LL NEVER TELL THE OTHER STUDENTS YOU KNOW WHY!
THE END

"A fairy curse," you say confidently.

The dragon doesn't move. He just looks at you sadly. You're beginning to feel a little nervous.

"Um . . . it might be a splinter, actually."

"Too late," says the dragon.

Yikes! You try to hop away from the dragon, but your frog body can't move fast enough. You feel the fiery breath from his nostrils right behind your back.

"My deepest apologies," says the dragon.

"Oh no, that's okay, I'll just leave right now—"

But the dragon opens his great mouth and swallows you in one gulp.

"Ha ha!" screeches the banshee. "It looks like you've reached . . .

THE END

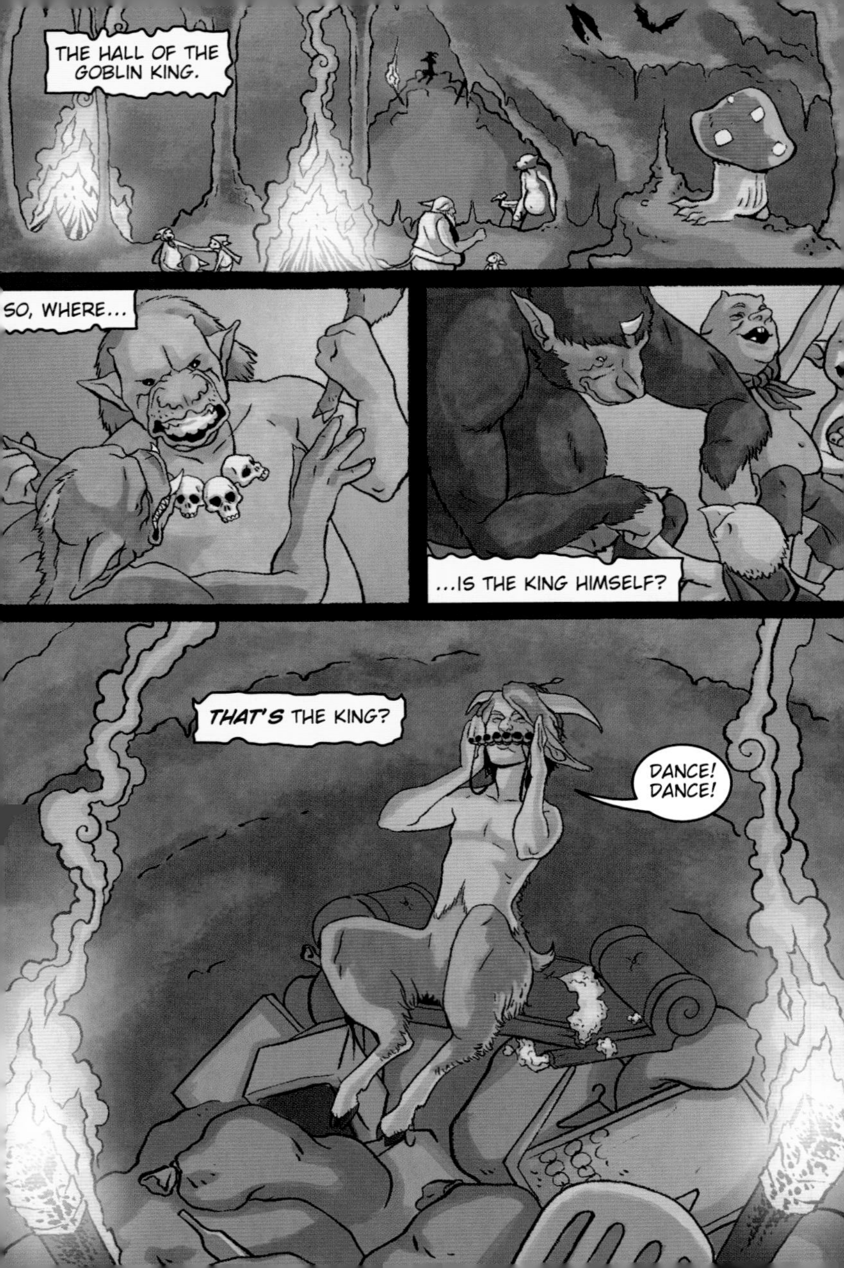
THE HALL OF THE GOBLIN KING.
SO, WHERE...
...IS THE KING HIMSELF?
THAT'S THE KING?
DANCE! DANCE!

You ask a nearby goblin just to make sure. "That hobgoblin over there . . . he's definitely the Goblin King?"

"Oh yes, that's our Robin Goodfellow, all right. He used to be Titania's servant. Then he decided to help free us all! Those fairies don't care for anyone but themselves. Would you like to meet him?"

Before you can even nod, the goblin waves at the king from across the cave.

"Robin! This fella wants to speak to you."

The king climbs down from his mountain of trash and walks over. "I see you're under a spell," he says.

"Titania did it."

He nods. "And you want me to reverse it? Well, I just might. If you fight in our battle tonight, I'll break the spell."

You hesitate. A battle sounds dangerous.

"Or if fighting scares you, you could wait here and dance," he says. He plays a little tune on his pipes and smiles.

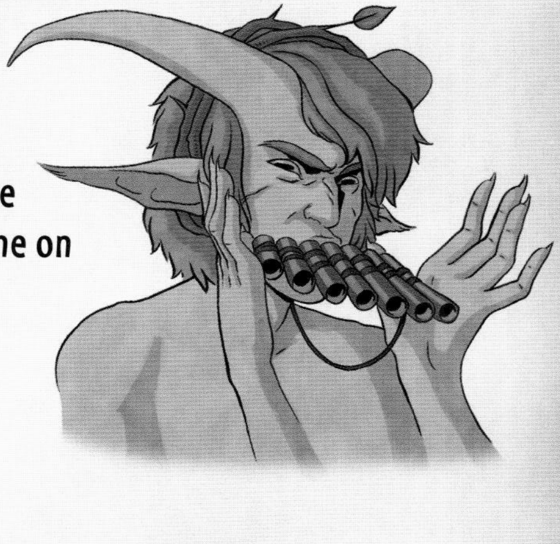

TURN TO PAGE 62.

It takes all of your courage, but you stay still as the red cap walks closer. His cap drips on the ground behind him. His hands are curled into claws with long, razor-sharp nails.

"I'm a frog," you say.

The red cap stops. "Why . . . so you are. But you do have blood, and my cap is getting a bit dry . . ."

"Oh, *my* blood is green."

"But what kind of frog talks? There's a spell on you."

"Why don't you break the spell and check?" you say.

The red cap waves his hands in the air. Suddenly, you find yourself on hands and knees on the ground.

"Human!" he shouts.

You scramble to open the gate and roll underneath it. The red cap's shouts fade as you run away. You look up and see the sun rising—good thing too, since you know that the inn is on the eastern side of the island.

You hurry back to Ms. Fraser. After all, you don't want to miss the tour tomorrow.

THE END

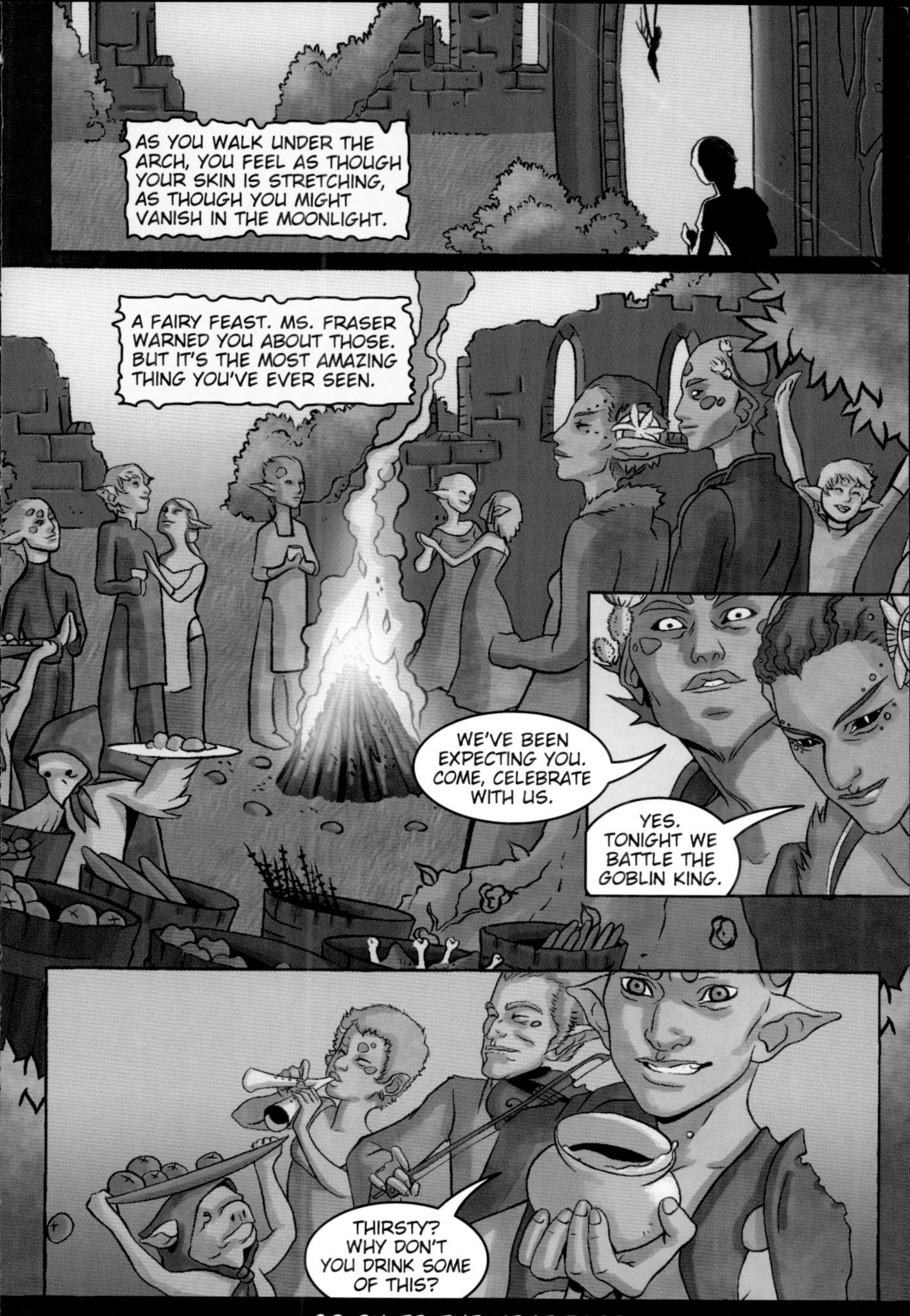
AS YOU WALK UNDER THE ARCH, YOU FEEL AS THOUGH YOUR SKIN IS STRETCHING, AS THOUGH YOU MIGHT VANISH IN THE MOONLIGHT.
A FAIRY FEAST. MS. FRASER WARNED YOU ABOUT THOSE. BUT IT'S THE MOST AMAZING THING YOU'VE EVER SEEN.
WE'VE BEEN EXPECTING YOU. COME, CELEBRATE WITH US.
YES. TONIGHT WE BATTLE THE GOBLIN KING.
THIRSTY? WHY DON'T YOU DRINK SOME OF THIS?

GO ON TO THE NEXT PAGE.

You *are* pretty thirsty. Hungry and tired too. And whatever's in that goblet smells like the best dessert you've ever had.

WILL YOU...

... drink it? What's the worst that could happen?
TURN TO PAGE 99.

... politely say no? Ms. Fraser warned you about fairy feasts.
TURN TO PAGE 51.

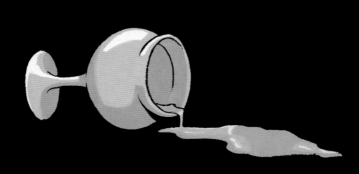

You blow on the sea horn as hard as you can. The sound is loud and clear, like a trumpet, and the Kelpie freezes in the ocean. The other kids are terrified, but you push through them to reach the Kelpie. You grab your two fellow students and pull them off the Kelpie's back. Then you rip away the seaweed tying Ms. Fraser to the Kelpie's neck. She swims around you and the other students, barking.

At first you think she's just happy to see the others rescued, but too late, you realize it's a warning! You look up right before a huge wave crashes over you. The sea horn falls out of your hand. Immediately, the Kelpie gallops away beneath the dark waves.

"It's gone!" says one of the students. "You saved us!"

"What's that seal doing over there?" says another.

You look and see a selkie leaping and yelping in the waves. Is she smiling at you? You grin but stay quiet. Ms. Fraser would want you to keep her secret.

THE END

You leap for Puck, knocking the Ever-Blooming Branch out of his hand. You grab the branch with your tongue and swallow it whole before he can stop you. Robin Goodfellow shakes the vines from his neck and lifts his weapon.

"Do you surrender?" he asks.

Puck growls. Up ahead, Titania shouts as she gallops toward you. Suddenly, heavy footsteps echo over the battlefield. The branch in your stomach starts to shake and jump. You look up into a leaf-covered face: the Green Man the fairies told you about.

"You control the Ever-Blooming Branch. What do you wish me to do?" he says in a booming voice.

"Help the Goblin King win!" you shout.

Immediately, the ground beneath the fairy army erupts with trees and flowers. Some fairies shriek as they're carried high above the ground on tree limbs. Other fairies' swords are snatched away by bushes. Puck knocks  aside Robin Goodfellow and runs away with the fairies, following Oberon and Titania.

You look around and all you see are joyous goblins and their kin. You've won the battle.

TURN TO PAGE 85.

Lead an army? That sounds tough. Maybe you should try to guess his name wrong. He does remind you of someone you once read about in class.

WILL YOU SAY...

. . . Puck?
TURN TO PAGE 8.

. . . Robin Goodfellow?
TURN TO PAGE 105.

The Shellyback looks you up and down and then slides off his pile of broken shells.

"Shellyback doesn't know what a human wants with him," he says. His voice sounds like a cat with a throat full of sand.

"I have a shell for you," you say.

"Then show it, show it."

You hand him the sea horn. The Shellyback leaps up in delight. His great shell cape clatters and scrapes. "Most excellent, excellent. You gets a fine reward, yes."

He turns around and begins to dig through his pile of shells, muttering to himself all the while. "Where did I put it, where?" he says. He turns around, and in his hand, you see a huge, fat earthworm. "Your reward!"

A worm? It's still *wiggling*. "Maybe I could just get a—"

"Yes, you are pleased, I know. No need to thank."

Oh well. You shrug and take the worm.

GO ON TO THE NEXT PAGE.

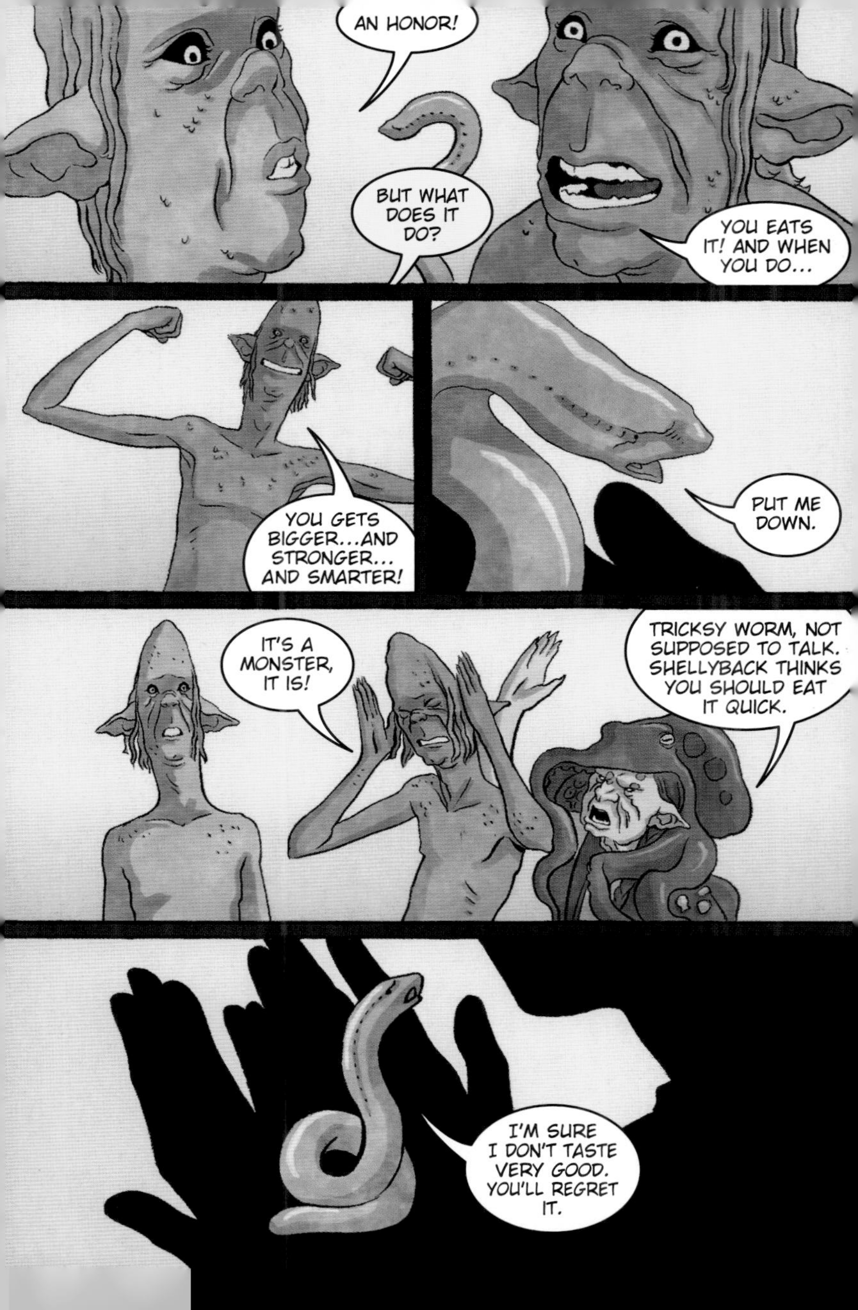
AN HONOR!
BUT WHAT DOES IT DO?
YOU EATS IT! AND WHEN YOU DO...
YOU GETS BIGGER...AND STRONGER... AND SMARTER!
PUT ME DOWN.
IT'S A MONSTER, IT IS!
TRICKSY WORM, NOT SUPPOSED TO TALK. SHELLYBACK THINKS YOU SHOULD EAT IT QUICK.
I'M SURE I DON'T TASTE VERY GOOD. YOU'LL REGRET IT.

Eww, eat a worm?
But it might be worse if you don't.
WILL YOU...

...hold your nose and eat it?
TURN TO PAGE 109.

...drop it on the ground?
TURN TO PAGE 102.

Robin Goodfellow looks at the retreating fairy army.

"You have saved my life, brave frog," he says. "And you have won our battle. From now on, the fairies must treat us as equals!"

The creatures on the plain jump and shout with joy.

"The moon is nearly set," he continues. "We must return to our world. And you must return to yours. But I made you a promise." He places his pitchfork on your head. For a moment, your skin feels hot enough to catch fire, and then you realize that you're human again.

"Good luck on your journey. Perhaps if you pass this way again, you'll leave some wine or bread for us, out of friendship with the goblins."

You promise. You want to say so much more, but Robin Goodfellow and his army start to fade as the sun rises.

You can go home, but you'll never forget the Goblin King.

THE END

You decide to ask Puck your own name.

"Y-your name?" Puck says. "Ahh . . . well . . ." He stamps his foot. "What kind of fairy knows human names?"

"You asked him yours," says Titania. "It's only fair."

"If I must, I name you . . . Will Shakespeare!"

You have to laugh. If you were William Shakespeare, you'd have a much easier time in English class.

"Puck, go to the cave and fetch the Ever-Blooming Branch," says Titania. "I think it should be ready by now."

Puck vanishes right before your eyes and reappears a few seconds later. Only now his hands are covered in slime.

He hands you a small branch with flowers all over it. "I had to fetch it from a frog. Use it well."

"What does it do?" you ask.

"Whoever holds it controls the Green Man, the most powerful creature of Tir na nOg. He has the power of life itself."

Oberon hands you a bundle of thistles sharp as a sword. "Tonight, you will lead the fairy army against Robin Goodfellow, the Goblin King!"

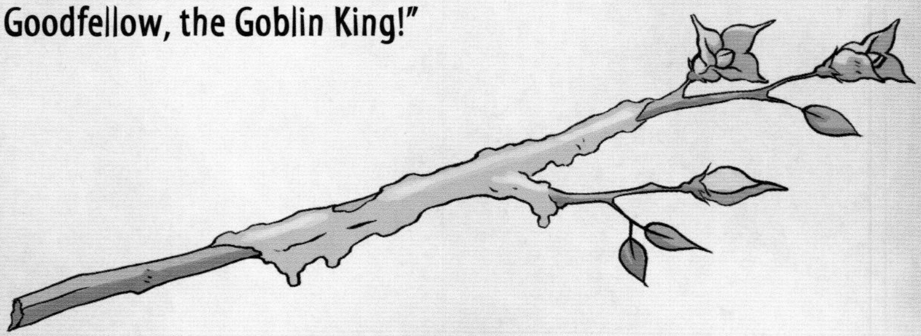

GO ON TO THE NEXT PAGE.

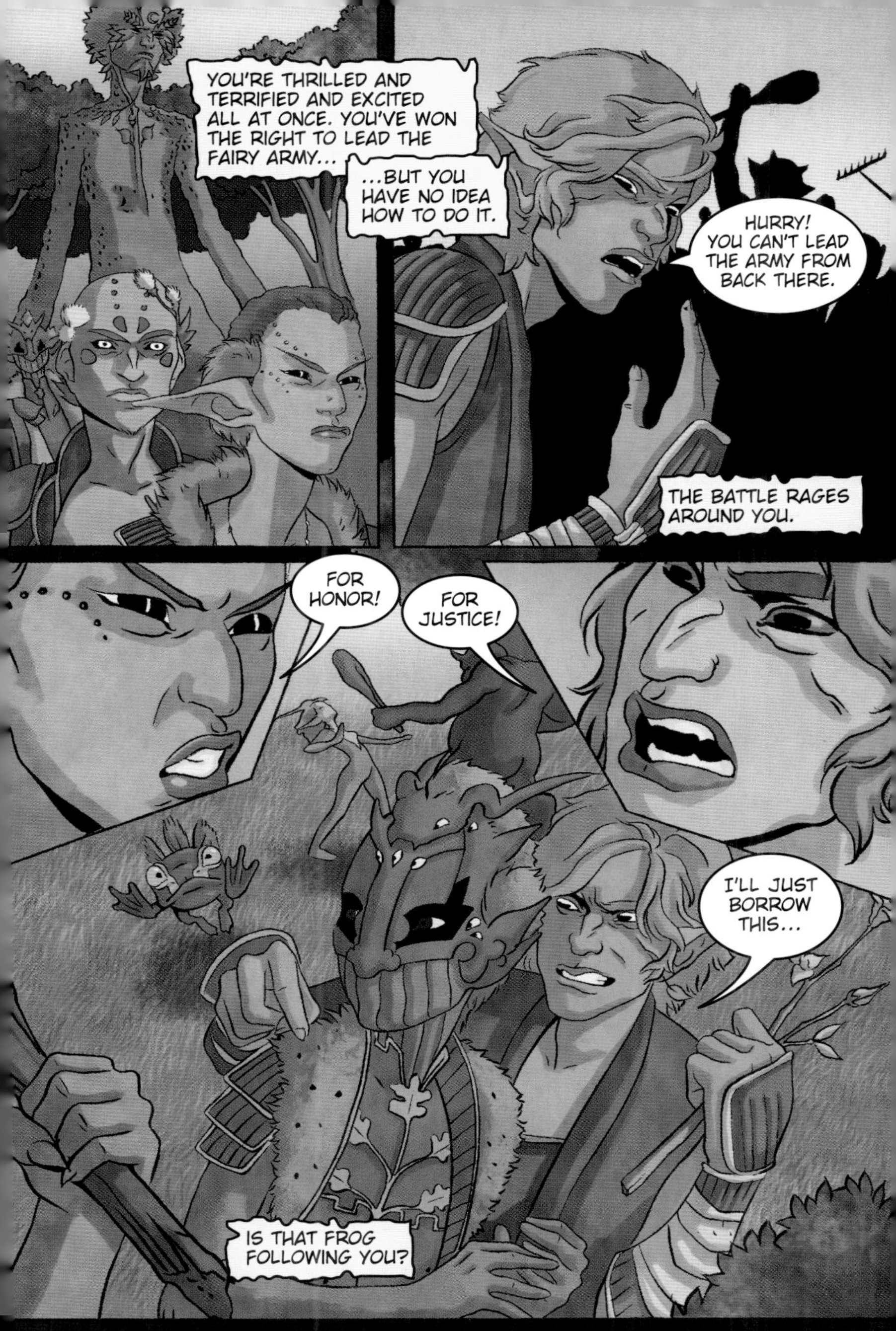
YOU'RE THRILLED AND TERRIFIED AND EXCITED ALL AT ONCE. YOU'VE WON THE RIGHT TO LEAD THE FAIRY ARMY...
...BUT YOU HAVE NO IDEA HOW TO DO IT.
HURRY! YOU CAN'T LEAD THE ARMY FROM BACK THERE.
THE BATTLE RAGES AROUND YOU.
FOR HONOR!
FOR JUSTICE!
I'LL JUST BORROW THIS...
IS THAT FROG FOLLOWING YOU?

GO ON TO THE NEXT PAGE.

WILL YOU...

...chase after Puck and take back the
Ever-Blooming Branch?
TURN TO PAGE 94.

...go after the frog?
Something about it looks weirdly familiar.
TURN TO PAGE 33.

...help fight in the battle as best you can?
TURN TO PAGE 20.

"No, Ms. Fraser, I can't let him kill you!"

You rip apart the seaweed tying her to the seafloor, ignoring her when she begs you to escape. You refuse to be a coward.

"What's this?" asks the Kelpie from behind you. "Another treat? A stowaway?"

You finally break the last of the knots, letting Ms. Fraser swim free. You try to swim with her, but something hard hits you from behind.

"*Not* a very smart idea," says the Kelpie.

Your head hurts, and you try to find the coin in your pocket. With Ms. Fraser gone, you can't breathe.

The Kelpie grins, showing its big, bloody teeth. "I think you're an even better meal than your little friend. Say good-bye . . ."

Ms. Fraser tries to smack the Kelpie with her tail, but it's too late.

You hope your parents will recognize your liver.

THE END

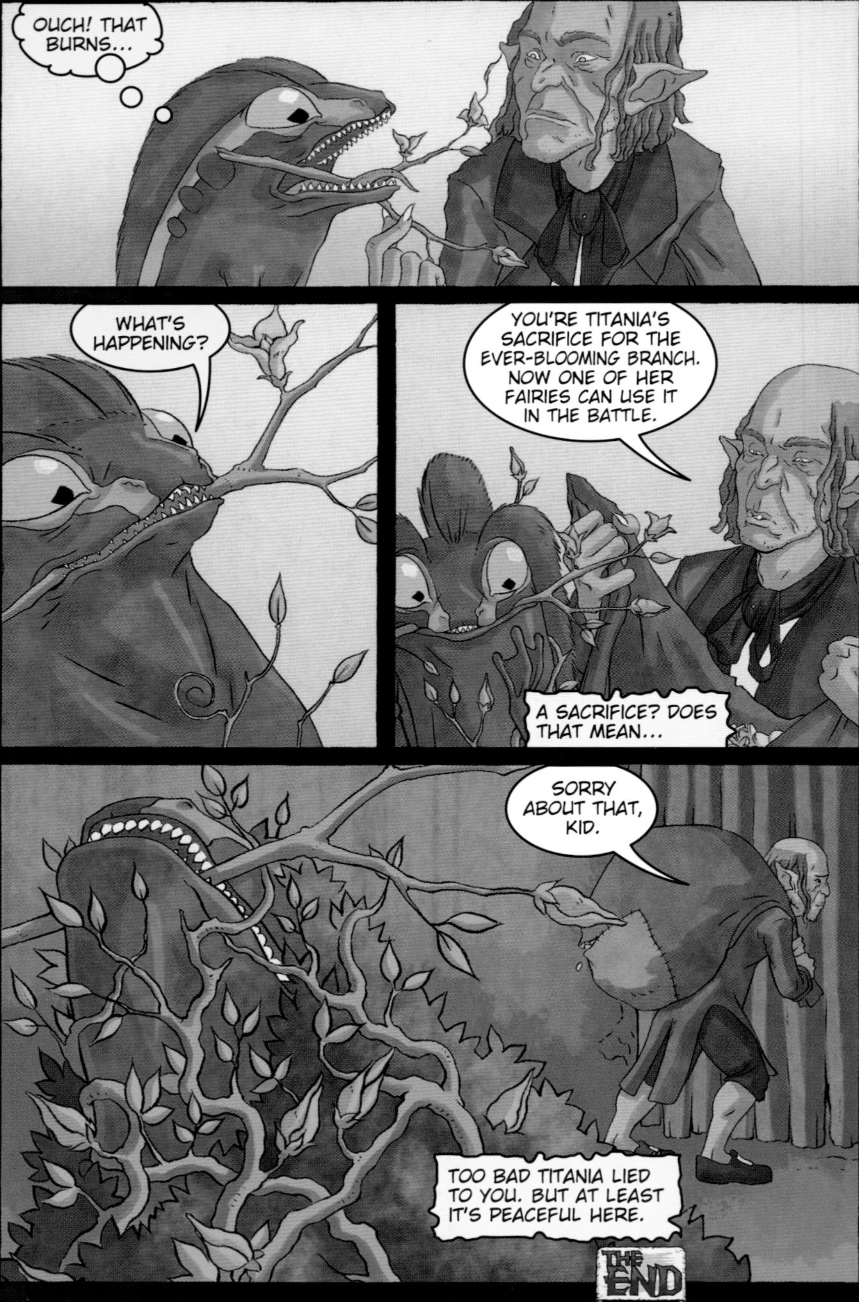
OUCH! THAT BURNS...
WHAT'S HAPPENING?
YOU'RE TITANIA'S SACRIFICE FOR THE EVER-BLOOMING BRANCH. NOW ONE OF HER FAIRIES CAN USE IT IN THE BATTLE.
A SACRIFICE? DOES THAT MEAN...
SORRY ABOUT THAT, KID.
TOO BAD TITANIA LIED TO YOU. BUT AT LEAST IT'S PEACEFUL HERE.
THE END

The brownie reaches into his bag and hands you a big mushroom.

"This will show you the way. Remember, Robin Goodfellow values a fighter."

The brownie sets off through the woods, leaving you alone. You stare at the mushroom. It has a red cap with white spots. How is this supposed to show you the way? Should you eat it? You start to put it in your mouth.

"Noooo!"

You drop the mushroom. To your surprise, it stands up on two little legs.

"Sorry," you say. "Could you take me to the Goblin King?"

The mushroom nods its big head and begins to walk down the dirt path. You follow and soon hear the sound of waves. Sure enough, it leads you to a tunnel in the sea cliffs. As you go deeper under the earth, it falls down and staggers back and forth across the path, giggling. You start to wonder if it has any idea where you're going.

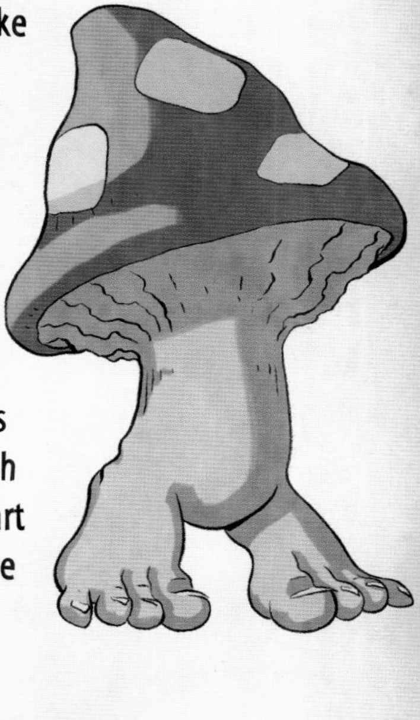

TURN TO PAGE 39.

You hop past the banshee and push open the door with your nose. Suddenly, you're in the bottom of a green valley covered in wildflowers and dozens of silver pieces. And is that a ruby shimmering in the moonlight?

If you could take all of this back home, you'd be rich for the rest of your life. You try to pick up some of it, but frog hands aren't any use at all. You drop each coin as soon as you pick it up.

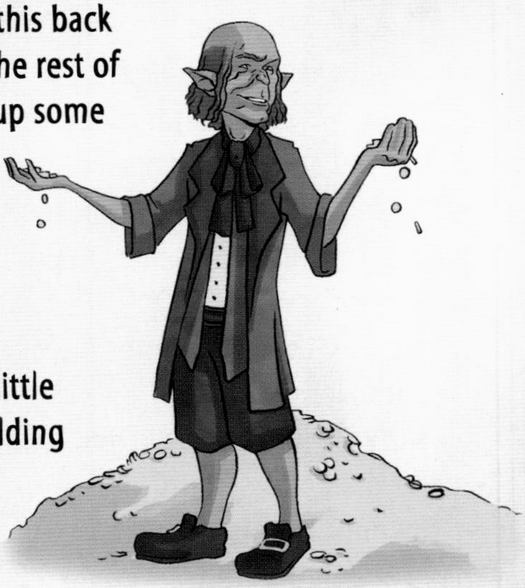

"Searching for this?"

You look up and see a little man dressed in green holding up a white branch. It's covered in pink and blue flowers. Surely this must be the Ever-Blooming Branch!

"You want this silly branch? When you could be rich?" he asks. "I'll let you keep every piece of silver you can hold in your mouth."

All that silver *does* look tempting. But maybe the little green man is acting *too* friendly . . .

GO ON TO THE NEXT PAGE.

You're learning not to trust
anyone in Tir na nOg.

WILL YOU...

. . . take the Ever-Blooming Branch,
trusting that Titania will change you back?
TURN TO PAGE 90.

. . . take the money?
Being a millionaire sure would be nice.
TURN TO PAGE 63.

"Come back!" you shout, but Puck has already vanished into the battle. How dare he steal the branch that you rightfully won? The thistle is sharp and strong, just like a sword. You use it to fight the goblins while you search for Puck. Finally, you hear a deep voice scream Puck's name across the battlefield. You run toward the sound. Sure enough, you soon see Puck desperately fighting with a hobgoblin you guess is Robin Goodfellow. Puck is on the ground, about to lose, but he holds the Ever-Blooming Branch above his head. Immediately, vines grow from it and start strangling the Goblin King. Puck laughs as the hobgoblin sinks to his knees.

But then something strange happens: The same giant frog you saw earlier leaps at Puck, knocking the Ever-Blooming Branch from his hands. Freed, Robin Goodfellow grabs his pitchfork and pierces Puck through the heart.

GO ON TO THE NEXT PAGE.

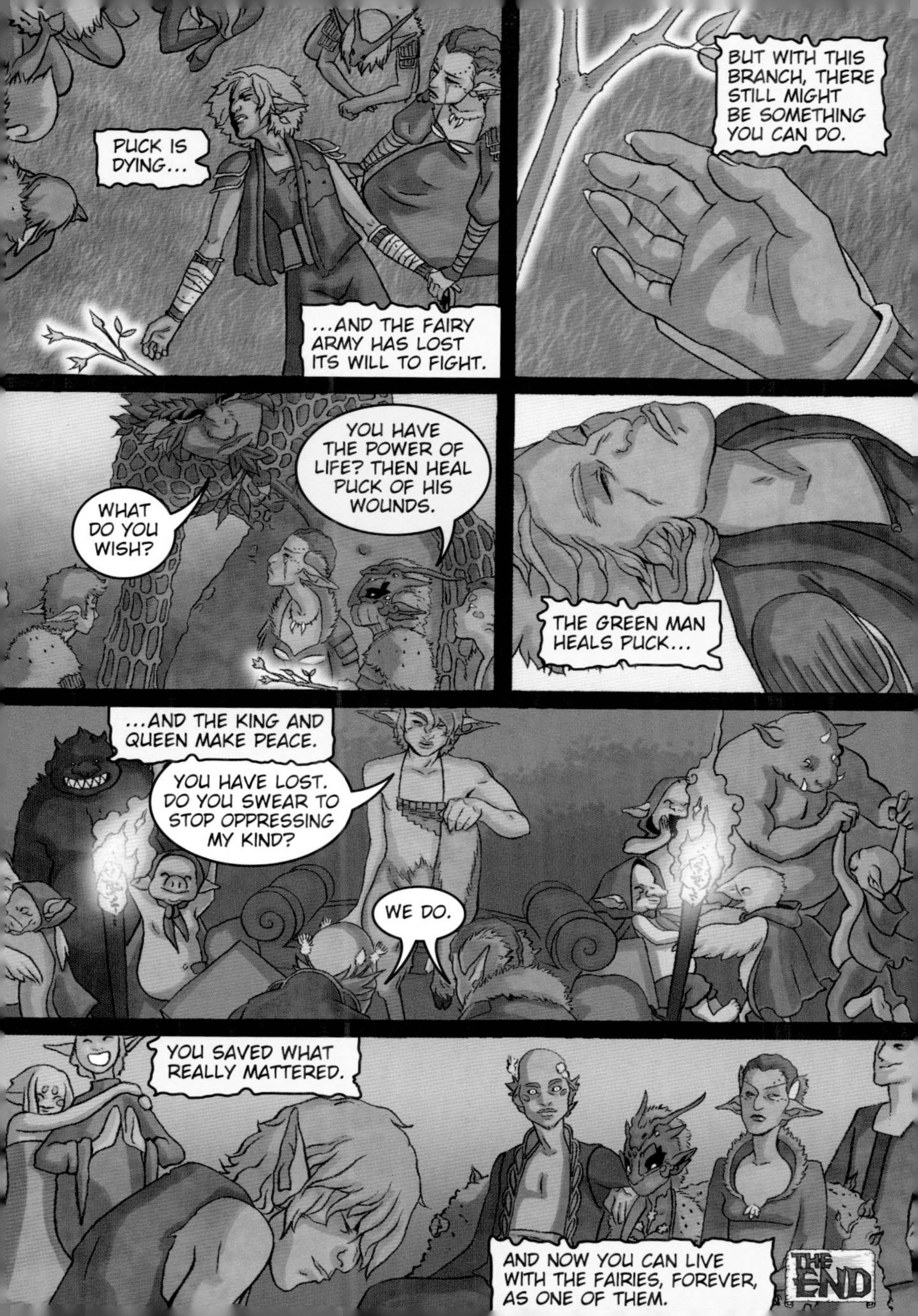
PUCK IS DYING...
...AND THE FAIRY ARMY HAS LOST ITS WILL TO FIGHT.
BUT WITH THIS BRANCH, THERE STILL MIGHT BE SOMETHING YOU CAN DO.
WHAT DO YOU WISH?
YOU HAVE THE POWER OF LIFE? THEN HEAL PUCK OF HIS WOUNDS.
THE GREEN MAN HEALS PUCK...
...AND THE KING AND QUEEN MAKE PEACE.
YOU HAVE LOST. DO YOU SWEAR TO STOP OPPRESSING MY KIND?
WE DO.
YOU SAVED WHAT REALLY MATTERED.
AND NOW YOU CAN LIVE WITH THE FAIRIES, FOREVER, AS ONE OF THEM.
THE END

The Finman, Mog and Cob tell you, is a mysterious creature. He can live on land or sea, and his handsome face has lured many humans to despair. If he catches people fishing in his territory, he will turn over their boats and drown them.

"But if he hates humans so much, why will he help me?" you ask.

"Because he likes the selkies, he does," says Mog.

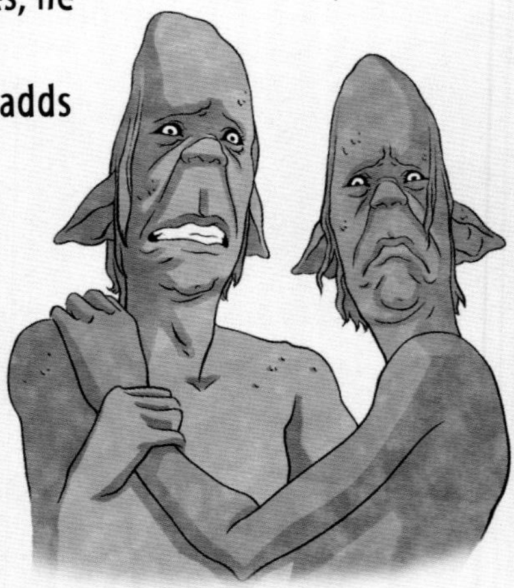

"And he hates the Kelpie," adds Cob.

"What kind of name is Finman, anyway?" you ask.

Cob puts his hand over your mouth. "Oh, don't you say that word!"

"We don't have names, not to a human!"

"Wait a second—I know your names!"

Mog covers his face with his hands. "We knows, it's terrible. You must never speak them, or we would have to leave. It's banishing, for ones of you to name ones of us."

You're surprised. You had no idea names had such power.

You hear a distant roaring and splash, like two giants are fighting nearby. What could it be?

GO ON TO THE NEXT PAGE.

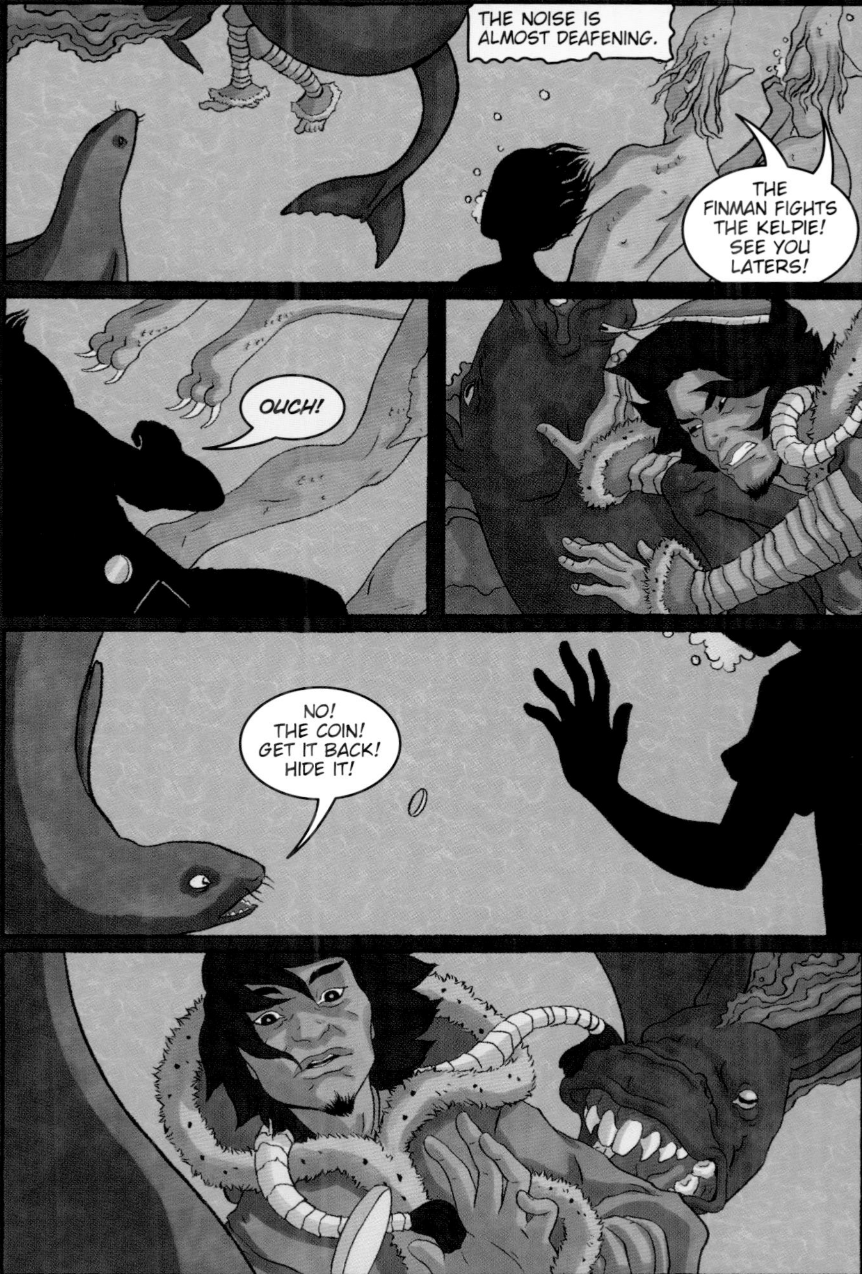
THE NOISE IS ALMOST DEAFENING.
THE FINMAN FIGHTS THE KELPIE! SEE YOU LATERS!
OUCH!
NO! THE COIN! GET IT BACK! HIDE IT!

GO ON TO THE NEXT PAGE.

There's no time to waste.

WILL YOU...

...grab the silver? You don't understand why, but it seems important to Ms. Fraser.
TURN TO PAGE 45.

...attack the Kelpie? You have only a spoon, but it's better than nothing.
TURN TO PAGE 37.

...name them all? You remember what the sea trows said about the power of names.
TURN TO PAGE 25.

You grab the goblet and drink it all in one gulp. It tastes like honey and peaches and a vanilla milk shake. And now you don't even feel tired! You look up at the grinning fairy who offered you the drink.

"Delicious, isn't it?" he asks.

You try to answer, but the word that leaves your mouth sounds more like a croak. "What's happening?" you try to say.

Dozens of other fairies gather around you, laughing. You try to move backward, but your step turns into a hop. You can't speak, and now you can't walk? What was in that drink?

"Dance with us, little froggie!" one of the fairies says to you.

You hold your hand in front of your face. But it's not a hand anymore. It's green and webbed.

"Oh no!" you shout, but it sounds like a croak.

You've been turned into a frog!

TURN TO PAGE 70.

Ms. Fraser is about to be kidnapped by
that strange horse.

WILL YOU...

...grab its tail?
TURN TO PAGE 57.

...run back to the house and ask
the brownie what to do?
TURN TO PAGE 64.

The princess laughs. "Stupid human. A clam has a huge mouth for a door!"

You sigh. "Oh well. I guess I'll leave then."

You start to swim away, but the princess lets out a wail. "Mummy! Give me the spoon! Gimme!"

You have a bad feeling about this. You try to swim faster.

"Oh, just take it," says the queen, behind you.

Before you can blink, the little mermaid has ripped the spoon from your hand. Immediately, the water starts to burn in your throat. You're going to drown!

The queen swims in front of you. "Well, that won't do. Why didn't you say you couldn't breathe without it?"

For a moment, you're relieved.

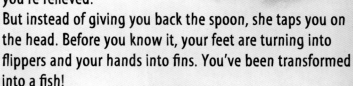

But instead of giving you back the spoon, she taps you on the head. Before you know it, your feet are turning into flippers and your hands into fins. You've been transformed into a fish!

"You can be my new friend, fishy," the princess says.

You think you're going to be here for a very long time.

THE END

No way are you going to eat a worm. Especially one that talks.

"Put me down," it says again.

Quickly, you place it on the bank beside the river.

"Good. Now walk widdershins around me three times."

You don't understand. "Widdershins?"

The worm sighs. "Counterclockwise. Do they teach you nothing in school?"

Well, you know which way a clock goes around. You walk around the worm three times in the opposite direction.

"Pick me up," says the worm. You lift him gently. He coughs ever so slightly. To your shock, a gold coin falls from his mouth and into your palm.

"Three times widdershins for gold," says the worm. "Now, aren't you glad you didn't eat me?"

You never stop regretting that you chose the worm over the horn that could save Ms. Fraser. Not even the money helps you forget your guilt. When you become the youngest millionaire in history, people wonder about the pet worm you keep in your office . . . and about the unhappiness that hangs over you like a dark cloud. They could never guess the truth.

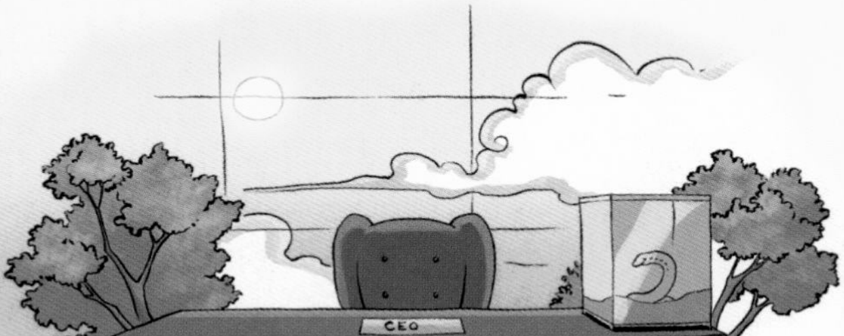
CEO

THE END

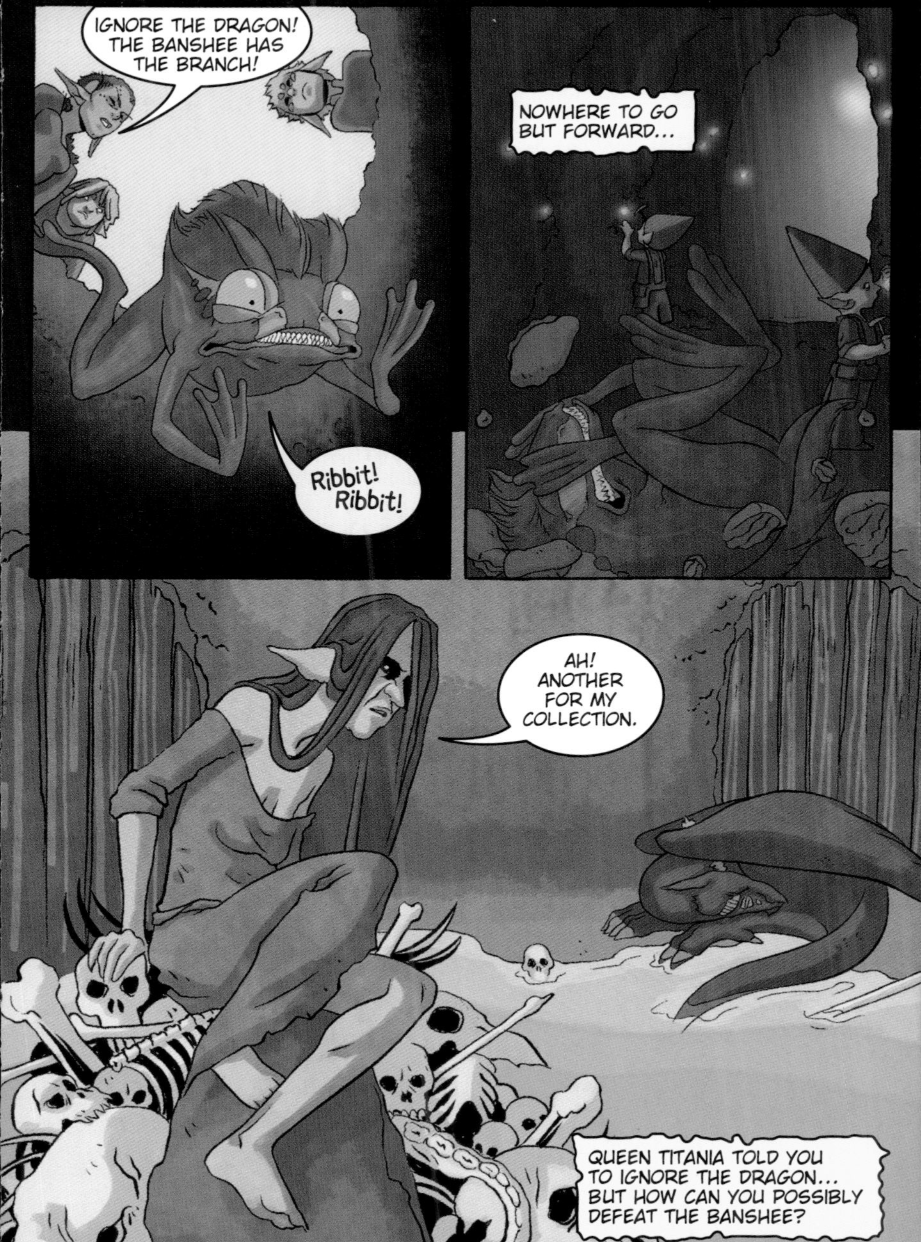
IGNORE THE DRAGON! THE BANSHEE HAS THE BRANCH!
Ribbit! Ribbit!
NOWHERE TO GO BUT FORWARD...
AH! ANOTHER FOR MY COLLECTION.
QUEEN TITANIA TOLD YOU TO IGNORE THE DRAGON... BUT HOW CAN YOU POSSIBLY DEFEAT THE BANSHEE?

GO ON TO THE NEXT PAGE.

The dragon sure looks a lot friendlier than the banshee. Then again, you might be a frog forever if you don't give Titania what she wants.

WILL YOU...

... screw up your courage and
approach the banshee?
TURN TO PAGE 38.

... ask the old dragon for help?
TURN TO PAGE 22.

"Robin Goodfellow."

Puck leaps from the table and lands before the fairy queen. "Aha! He gives me the name of my mortal enemy!"

The queen sighs. "Puck, I suppose you may lead the fight against Robin Goodfellow, the Goblin King."

King Oberon puckers his lips and blows. The air fills with a stream of glowing dust. A stem of thistle appears in the air before Puck. The little elf snatches up the thistle and holds it above his head like a sword.

"To battle, fairies!" he shouts.

You aren't really sure you wanted to lead the army anyway, but you feel a little left out. The queen ruffles your hair.

"And you, my sweet changeling child, can play the merry pipes for the soldiers."

She hands you a set of long silver pipes bound together with rough string. You aren't sure how to use them, but it sounds a lot better than fighting with thistles!

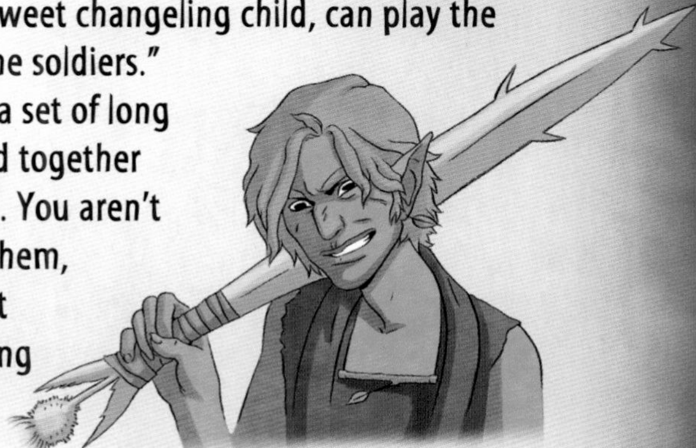

GO ON TO THE NEXT PAGE.

With cheers and shouts, the fairy army leaves the ruins. The other musicians start to walk with you off to the side of the main army. There's a young girl fairy playing a flute and an old man carrying a fiddle.

"Try playing, child," says the old man. "The army needs our song."

You feel nervous. "I don't know how . . ."

The girl laughs. "Oh, but you're the royal child! Music is in your blood. Try, you'll see."

So you place the pipes to your lips and start to blow. To your surprise, they seem as familiar to you as if you had been playing your whole life. You laugh and play a bit of a song you heard earlier, at the fairy feast. The girl jumps in with her flute, and the old man joins with his fiddle. Soon the whole fairy army is leaping and singing on their way to the battlefield.

TURN TO PAGE 67.

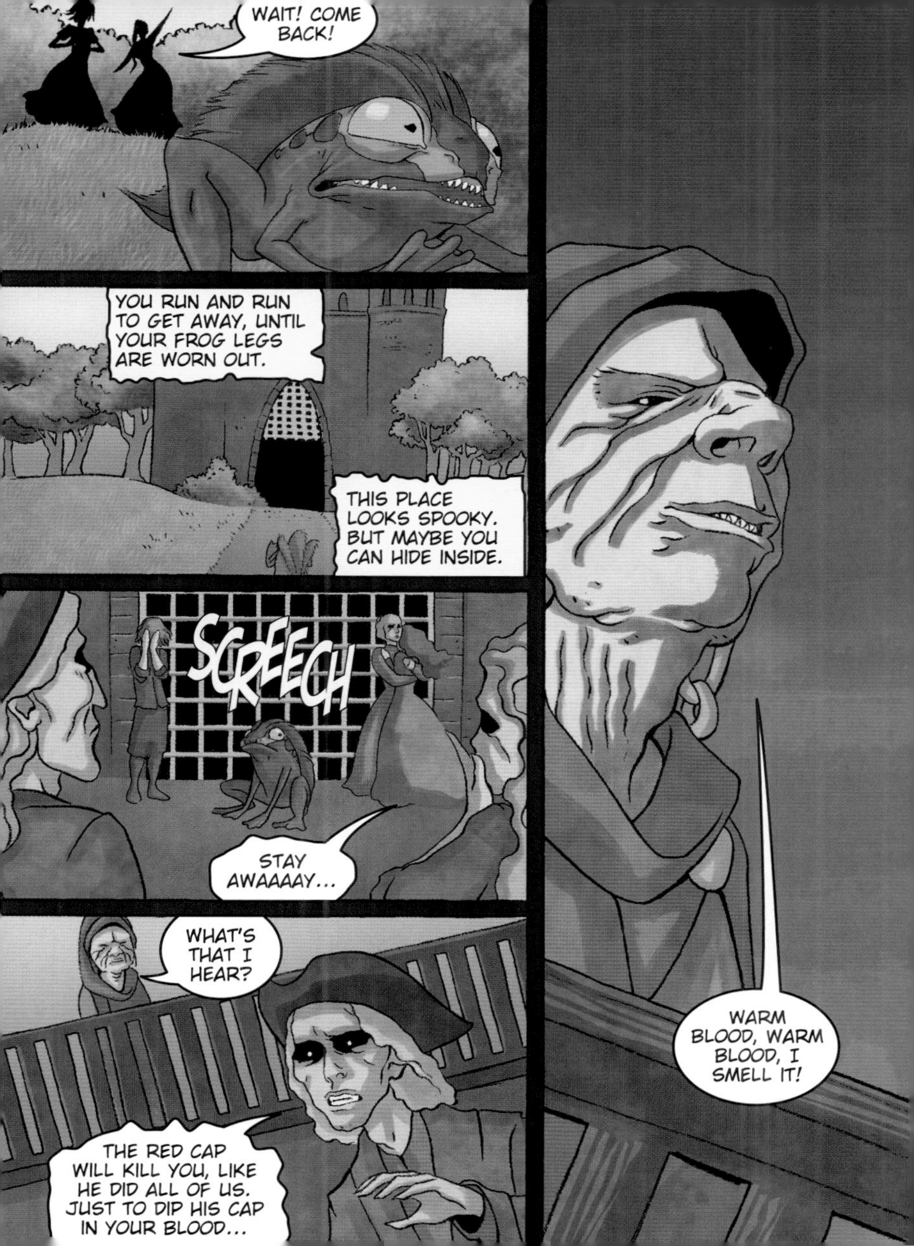
WAIT! COME BACK!
YOU RUN AND RUN TO GET AWAY, UNTIL YOUR FROG LEGS ARE WORN OUT.
THIS PLACE LOOKS SPOOKY. BUT MAYBE YOU CAN HIDE INSIDE.
SCREECH
STAY AWAAAAY...
WHAT'S THAT I HEAR?
THE RED CAP WILL KILL YOU, LIKE HE DID ALL OF US. JUST TO DIP HIS CAP IN YOUR BLOOD...
WARM BLOOD, WARM BLOOD, I SMELL IT!

This guy *really* doesn't like uninvited guests.

WILL YOU...

... find the nearest closet and hide?
Maybe dust will hide the smell of
your "warm blood."
TURN TO PAGE 69.

... try to trick him?
Being a frog has to be good for *something*.
TURN TO PAGE 76.

"This is a bad idea," says the worm.

The sea trows might be the stupidest creatures in Tir na nOg, but you don't think you should trust a worm either. You close your eyes and suck down the worm like a noodle.

"You'll be sorry!" the worm shouts as he slides down your throat.

"What's he taste like?" Mog asks. "Mutton? Liver? Crickets?"

Your stomach feels funny. You wonder if you might vomit. "I don't feel too good . . ."

You try to stand straight, but your legs won't move properly. And your face feels all funny too.

"Runs away, runs away!" screams Cob, suddenly. "It's a hobgoblin trickster, come to steal your rewards!"

The sea trows leap into the river and swim out of sight. The Shellyback runs into the hills, his cape clattering behind him. You dare to look at yourself in the water. You've been turned into a hobgoblin.

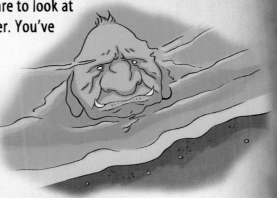

You can hear the worm from inside your belly. "Told you so," it says.

THE END

You take a deep, froggy breath. "A splinter?" you say.

For a moment, you're terrified that you gave the wrong answer. But instead of breathing fire at you, the dragon tosses his head. The flowers fall to the ground in a shower of petals. He lets out a huge roar.

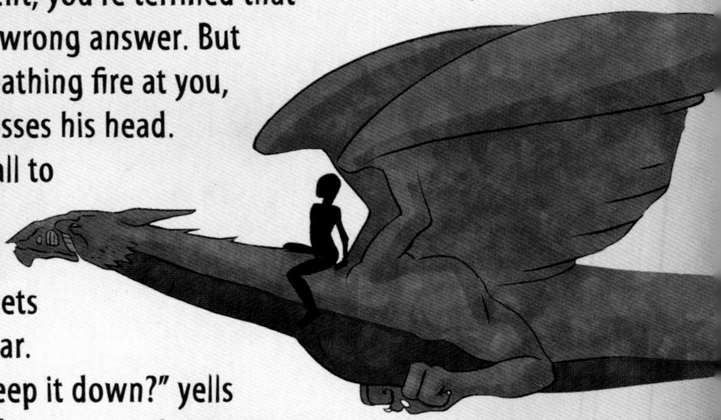

"Will you keep it down?" yells the banshee from across the cave.

"My apologies," says the dragon.

He turns to you and opens his mouth. *Now* is he going to burn you to a crisp? No! Instead of fire, you are engulfed in a stream of light. When the light fades, you've become human again.

"Oh, thank you!" you exclaim. "But how do I get back to the inn . . . ?"

"Open the door," says the dragon, "and I shall take you."

As you soar through the night on the back of a dragon, you know that this has been an adventure you will never forget.

THE END

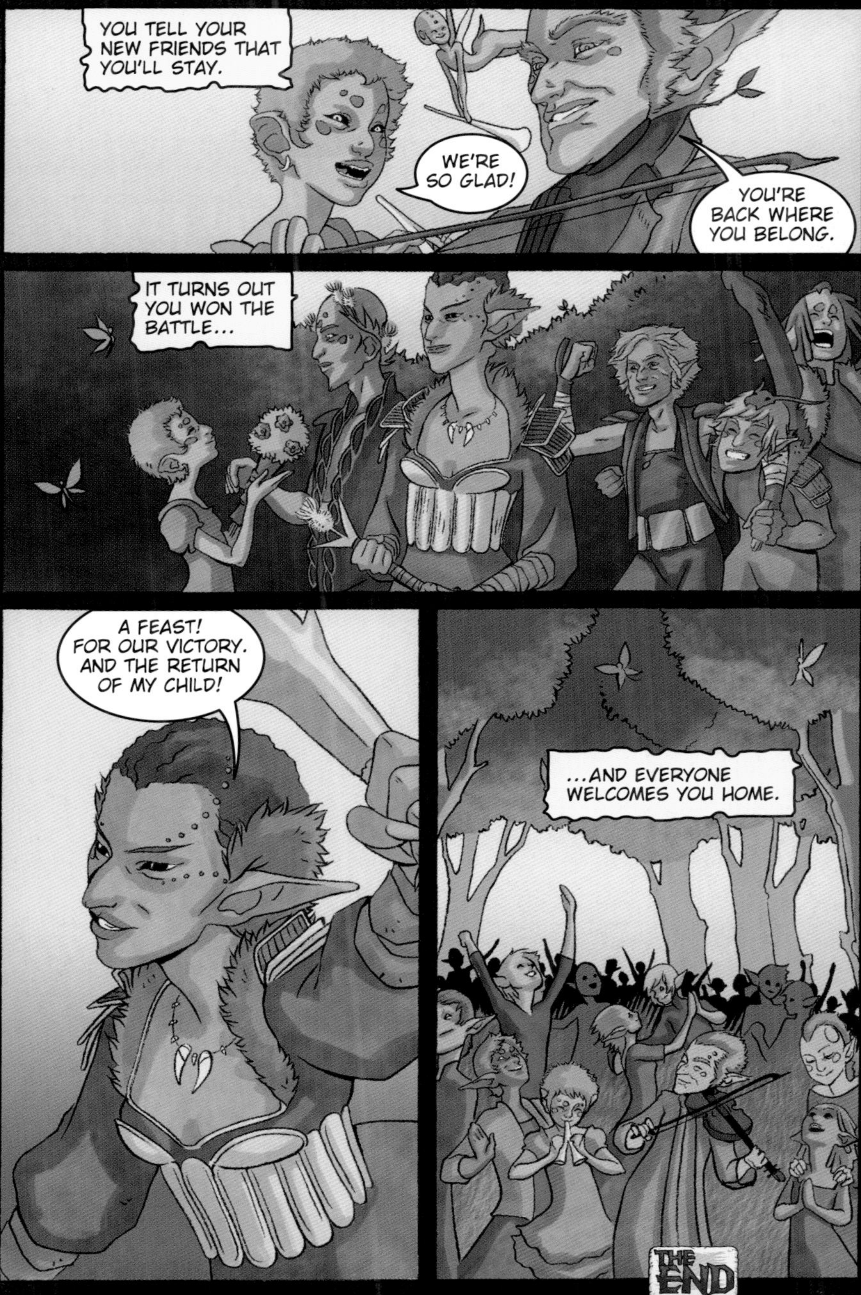
YOU TELL YOUR NEW FRIENDS THAT YOU'LL STAY.
WE'RE SO GLAD!
YOU'RE BACK WHERE YOU BELONG.
IT TURNS OUT YOU WON THE BATTLE...
A FEAST! FOR OUR VICTORY. AND THE RETURN OF MY CHILD!
...AND EVERYONE WELCOMES YOU HOME.
THE END

WHICH TWISTED JOURNEYS® WILL YOU TRY NEXT?

#1 CAPTURED BY PIRATES
Can you keep a band of scurvy pirates from turning you into shark bait?

#2 ESCAPE FROM PYRAMID X
Not every ancient mummy stays dead . . .

#3 TERROR IN GHOST MANSION
The spooks in this Halloween house aren't wearing costumes . . .

#4 THE TREASURE OF MOUNT FATE
Can you survive monsters and magic and bring home the treasure?

#5 NIGHTMARE ON ZOMBIE ISLAND
Will you be the first to escape Zombie Island?

#6 THE TIME TRAVEL TRAP
Danger is everywhere when you're caught in a time machine!

#7 VAMPIRE HUNT
Vampire hunters are creeping through an ancient castle. And you're the vampire they're hunting!

#8 ALIEN INCIDENT ON PLANET J
Make peace with the Makaknuk, Zirifubi, and Frongo, or you'll never get off their planet . . .

#9 AGENT MONGOOSE AND THE HYPNO-BEAM SCHEME
Your top-secret mission, if you choose to accept it: foil the plots of an evil mastermind!

#10 THE GOBLIN KING
Will you join the fearsome goblins or the dangerous elves?